A my
Christmas, 2016

MR. SWENSEN

MR. SWENSEN

A Novel

I wish you enjoyment!

Paul Krebill
2016

Paul Krebill

ISBN: Softcover   978-1-5144-8750-1
             eBook   978-1-5144-8749-5

Print information available on the last page.

Rev. date: 05/20/2016

To order additional copies of this book, contact:
Xlibris
1-888-795-4274
www.Xlibris.com
Orders@Xlibris.com
732070

PROLOGUE

Reese Creek, Montana

The town of Reese Creek, founded by John Reese in 1864, is located about eighteen miles, as the crow flies, southeast of the place where Lewis and Clark discovered the headwaters of the Missouri River in 1805. In its heyday the town of Reese Creek boasted a church and a school as well as a general store, a blacksmith shop, and a cheese factory.

Now in what remains of Reese Creek, the Erickson house stands empty. Jeff Sumner farmed the Erickson place after Jon Erickson and his wife, Anna, died in the flu epidemic of 1918. Without adult heirs, the farm and the outbuildings were held in trust by the Security Bank of Bozeman from which the Sumners rented the farm. The only surviving family member was Karl, a five year old child for whom the bank would hold the property in trust until his twenty-first birthday.

When his parents both died of the flu epidemic, a sister of Karl Erickson's mother, who was living in Billings, took Karl under her care. In time she and her husband legally adopted Karl. This adoption of Karl was unknown to the bank at the time, nor in the years following. Amid the chaos which the flu epidemic brought about, neighbors in the community lost track of Karl or his whereabouts.

According to bank records, when Karl reached the age of majority in 1934 he would be ready to receive the inheritance. However, confusion over Karl's adoption and change of name resulted in the bank's losing track of Karl for a number of years. In the meantime Mr. and Mrs. Sumners continued to rent for a few more very difficult years due to extended periods of drought. An earthquake in 1925 caused significant damage to some of the buildings on the Erickson farm. Then in the winter of 1927 Both Mr. and Mrs. Summers were killed in a car accident when they slid on black ice into an oncoming vehicle. As a result, the farm fell into disuse; under the trusteeship held by the bank. Eventually the house and other buildings deteriorated into what appeared to be "ghost town" conditions with little or no supervision by the bank, and a declining population in the area surrounding the Erickson place.

PART ONE

*In which from time to time
Mr. Swensen writes the
story of his earlier life*

CHAPTER I

Elmhurst, Illinois–1948

Students were mounting the steps into Irion Hall on their way to the Friday morning chapel service, a daily attendance which Elmhurst College expected in those days. Most often such services were conducted by members of the faculty, many of whom were clergy. On this particular day in December, Mr. Swensen of the history department presided. John Schroeder, a student in the junior class, was the chapel organist. He was playing a Bach prelude as the students and faculty took their seats in the polished oak pews. After a hymn, and an opening prayer, and the scripture of the day, Mr. Swensen continued with a brief sermon.

"My subject today is *death and immortality*. I know this is an unusual consideration for people of college age and connection, but I have been aware of the fact that many of our newly enrolled students have recently been discharged from military service during the war. Some, with whom I have spoken have faced violent deaths on the battlefield and are in need of putting those harrowing experiences into perspective. Furthermore, as is true with many in my age group, I have faced untimely death more than once in my life. My own parents died in the Asian Flu epidemic in 1918 when I was only five years old. Thus, I have no memory of my natural mother and father, nor of the home in which I spent my earliest years. And then in later life I had to bid farewell to someone very close to me.

"In addition to our reading of I Corinthians 15, I would like to read portions of "Crossing the Bar," a poem by Alfred Tennyson.

> Sunset and evening star
> And one clear call for me!
> And may there be no moaning at the bar
> When I put out to sea.
> Twilight and evening bell!
> And after that the dark!
> And may there be no sadness of farewell
> When I embark.
> For though from far out our bourne of time and place
> The flood may bear me far,
> I hope to see my Pilot face to face,
> When I have crossed the bar.

"I personally have found the metaphor of the sea, as bearing one to a far off land, to be most helpful, in contemplating death."

Mr. Swensen continued with his sermon, expanding on the idea of the passage over the sea to heaven, with Jesus Christ as the ship's pilot. The sermon was followed with the hymn, "Jesus, Savior, Pilot Me," after which the congregation filed out of the chapel and out of Irion Hall to disperse to classes for the morning. Two of the returned veterans spoke with Mr. Swensen before leaving the room. One, who had been in the Navy, said to Mr. Swensen, "Your speaking of the sea as a way to comprehend death was very meaningful and helpful to me, sir. I served in the U.S.Navy on a battleship and often found myself overwhelmed by the sea itself."

"You did! Thank you for sharing with me. I'm glad I could be of some help."

That night, after their supper in the Commons, Dale Schmidt and Maynard Otterberg returned to their room in the men's dorm. Both had studies to do. Maynard asked Dale. "What did you think of Swensen's chapel this morning?"

"I don't know. He seemed different. . ."

"How so?"

"Very serious and in a way-- sad."

"I think I felt that way too, almost like he was conducting a funeral for someone he knew."

The two got out their books and began studying. After a while, Dale sighed in despair and shoved away from his desk. "I just don't understand this history assignment."

"Go see Swensen. They're always telling us that we are at a small college in which the faculty are available and want to give us help when we need it."

"Yeah. . . ."

"You know, all that talk about that's why a small college is best."

"It's not too late?"

"Nah. Go see Mr. Swensen. His office is upstairs in Old Main."

"Okay Maynard. You talked me into it."

A short while later Dale returned. "He wasn't there. Won't be until Monday."

"How do you know that?"

"A sign on his door says. . . *Back on Monday.*"

"Yeah, I heard somebody else found out one time that he was gone for the weekend."

"Wonder where he goes. I don't think he has any relatives around here."

"Seems like a lonely bachelor. . . a mysterious one at that, I'd say."

CHAPTER II

Darkness was coming early on that October Friday. The temperature had dipped into the twenties, when Mr. Swensen locked the door of his rooms on the third floor of Old Main and went down the side stairway to step out onto the campus. He was alone as he drew his long overcoat around him and adjusted his black fedora to shield as much of his head from the cold as possible. No one saw him walk off the campus and downtown to the Chicago Northwestern Railroad depot.

The conductor greeted him as he stepped up into the coach. "Hello, Mr. Swensen." He acknowledged the greeting and took his seat alone and peered out the window watching the familiar sights go by, while the train resumed its run into the Northwestern Station in downtown Chicago where he stepped down from the coach.

He made his way to the northbound bus on Michigan Boulevard and boarded it. After a short ride he was soon descending the step onto the sidewalk to walk to Lake Shore Drive to a tall high-rise which he entered. The uniformed doorman greeted him, "Hello, Mr. Swensen."

"Good evening, George."

When the elevator door closed behind Mr. Swensen, the security guard walked over to the doorman. "What do you know about him?"

"Nothing, really. I see him every Friday when he comes in like he did just now, and then he comes and goes over the weekend. But he is never here after Sunday afternoon until the next Friday."

"Where is he the rest of the week? Do you know?"

"No, not really."

"Any idea?"

"I think he's a professor somewhere."

"How long's he been here?"

"At least as long as I've been working here."

"A mystery man. . .but he's not a security problem, so I guess it's none of my business."

"You're right."

An elevator took Karl Swensen to the sixteenth floor. He took out his key as he approached Room 1619.

Upstairs in 1619, as was his custom, he did not turn on the lights, but went instead to his chair by the large window, sat down to look out over the black silver-shimmering lake on yet another Friday night. Later he would fix a simple meal for himself before retiring for the night.

On Saturday, the early morning sun and wind splashed the blue-gray waves of the lake with glowing golden laps, reflecting into his living room as Karl opened his drapes. Dressing casually for his Saturday routine he let himself out of his apartment and down the elevator to walk out of his building onto the street. The fresh air strewn with slight whiffs of the aroma of lake moisture was exhilarating.

It would be a good day with inspiration for his writing. He had selected his lake shore apartment as his get-away the ideal setting for writing the story of his earlier life. A block west and around, the corner was his favorite "downtown" café as he liked to call it. He was a regular. They all recognized him, yet knew little about him.

"Good morning, Mr. Swensen."

"Yes, good morning, Gloria."

"The usual?"

"Of course." He replied as he took his place at the counter and reached for the morning edition of the "Trib."

Soon his English muffin and orange marmalade appeared along with his poached egg and a pot of hot tea. Now his Saturday could begin in customary order.

After breakfast he paid his bill and returned to his apartment, where he would continue writing his story. It was his custom to sit at a simple writing desk before the tall window facing the lake. He wrote in longhand on lined paper in a three-ringed note book. He had no idea what form the finished account would take, or for whom it was intended. At this point he was writing to clarify his own story to seal it in his memory so that he could re-live his own happier days. *And perhaps for those who come after me. If they were to be interested,* he thought wistfully. And so he would continue his writing.

CHAPTER III

Mr. Swensen writes his story beginning 17 years earlier.

Chicago---November, 1931

I found a vacant seat in Hutchinson cafeteria and put my tray down, as the person beside my place finished his meal and left. The university cafeteria was always crowded during the noon break from classes. I happened to look up and spotted a familiar face as she entered. She was alone. I thought she was attractive, neatly dressed in a blue and green plaid skirt and white sweater. Her loosely curled brown hair and brown eyes gave a gentle impression. Of medium height, she carried herself somewhat cautiously. After filling her tray, she had begun looking for a seat. She noticed the vacancy next to me and appeared to recognize me. I recognized her as a student in the American Frontier Issues history class of the last hour.

"May I sit here?" she asked as she prepared to put her tray down next to me.

"Certainly. I am alone. I'm not expecting anyone."

"Thanks. This place is always crowded," she said as she put her tray down and took her seat next to me. She began to eat her lunch and then broke the silence. "What did you think of the lecture?"

"Well, to tell you the truth, I found it fascinating."

She thought for a moment. "I did too. . .by the way, I'm Elizabeth Burgess."

"Hello. My name's Karl Swensen."

We dove into our lunches at this point and were quiet. I felt ill at ease.

"Where are you from, Karl?"

"Montana."

"Oh wow. I've never known anybody from Montana."

"How about you?"

"Oh, I'm from just west of here in Elmhurst. It's a suburb about eight miles west of the city limits of Chicago. I grew up there and graduated from York High."

"Did you get your undergraduate degree here?"

"No, for college I stayed at home, since Elmhurst has a college. So I lived at home and walked up to the campus for my classes, and then home to study. . . not much social life." She appeared pensive. "Just continued in the home life I had enjoyed since childhood. . . Where did you do your undergraduate work?"

"I didn't have much social life either. I went to school in my own town also."

"Where was that?"

"Eastern Montana College in Billings where I grew up." I said under my breath. "But not much home life . . . ."

Neither of us seemed to know what next to say as we finished our lunches. She was the first to put her napkin on her tray and to stand up. She waited for me to do the same and I got the impression that she was waiting to leave the cafeteria together. So I stood and we put our trays in the tray cart and made for the door together.

Outside on the sidewalk we realized we needed to go in different directions. She smiled at me and said. "I enjoyed having lunch with you, Karl."

"It was good to meet you, Elizabeth. I'll probably see you in class on Wednesday."

"I hope so. Goodbye now."

"Bye." As I made my way to my room I felt a smile come upon my face and I thought to myself. *I hope so too.*

That night when I put my head on my pillow to begin my sleep, a fleeting image of Elizabeth's face appeared. Such a thing as that had never happened to me before. I woke up the next morning wishing it were Wednesday. But it was Tuesday and there were other classes on my schedule. Throughout the day I thought about Elizabeth every so often. There was something about the way she seriously wanted to become acquainted. She didn't appear to want to impress, as so many people do when one first meets them. I felt a warmth in the way she related to me. And this made me feel warmly toward her. I worried, however, wondering what, she was thinking of me, if anything. *Probably nothing.*

I had a lot of self-doubt in this sort of situation. My only somewhat serious relationship with a girl had been in high school. I was painfully shy and so had been very reluctant about asking a girl out. As a result, it turned out that it had been a girl who had asked me out. Wilma was in our Lutheran Church youth group and confirmation class, in which I also was a member. She had recently moved to Billings from Minot, North Dakota. We were both in the same high school class. She seemed to have few friends in her new school, and found herself talking to me frequently. We got along easily. She had the same religious background as I did and so when at the end of our junior year a school dance was announced, she asked me for a date, but not for the dance itself, because neither of our families approved of dancing. Our date was on the same night as the high school dance. Her parents provided a dinner for us at a nice restaurant at the Northern Hotel and suggested that we take in a movie afterward. In fact her father took us downtown in his car and picked us up after the movie. When we got to her house, Wilma's mother had some refreshments for us before I left for my house.

During the summer and into the next year we continued a friendly relationship, in confirmation class and at other times as well. I thought that perhaps after high school we might get serious about our relationship. . . until at Christmas break she announced that she would be spending two weeks back in Minot with her boyfriend. So ended our relationship.

This pretty much robbed me of my self-confidence when it came to my ability to appeal to persons of the opposite gender, making me now doubt that Elizabeth would continue to want to see me.

Wednesday finally arrived and I entered my American Frontiers class, eagerly awaiting to see Elizabeth again. But to my dismay she had not come to class. There were only fifteen or so students and so I could not have missed seeing her. After class I made my way to the cafeteria. I was disappointed that I would not be seeing Elizabeth. However, when I had gotten my tray and began looking for a seat, I was surprised to see her waving at me and pointing to the seat next to her.

I hurried over and put my tray down next to hers and exclaimed as I seated myself, "I didn't think I'd see you, since you weren't in class!"

"I know. I couldn't make it, but I didn't want to miss seeing you again, Karl."

"Same here. I was sorry when I didn't see you in class."

She smiled. "How was the class? What did I miss?"

"Oh, not much. I kept looking for you and I guess I was sort of distracted."

"My sakes! I hope I didn't derail your education." She said with a sly grin.

"Oh. I'll recover."

"Good. . . Tell me more about your growing up in Montana. I've never been west of the Mississippi. Your parents still there, I assume?"

"Well, no. . . not exactly. I lost my real parents to the 1918 flu epidemic when I was five years old. . . . that was on a farm in a little place called Reese Creek, near Bozeman.

"I'm sorry. That must have been hard for you."

"I don't know, because all of that was blocked out of my memory since I was only five at the time. My mother's sister and her husband had taken me out of the house where my parents were overcome with the flu, to keep me from catching the disease. They moved me in with them in Billings. At first on a temporary basis."

"Where was that?"

"About a half day's drive east of Reese Creek. . . anyway I never was taken back to the farm. My parents died soon after. So Billings became my permanent residence. They adopted me. I had almost no memory of anything earlier in my life. In fact, in my earlier years I did not even know I had been adopted. I didn't find that out until I was in high school It was a very difficult time for me as I got older and realized I didn't know what had happened."

"Only when you got older?

"I had only vague memories of my life before I was adopted."

"Did you have brothers or sisters?"

"No. As far as I know, I was an only child."

"That really left you alone."

"Billings, where I lived, is about a hundred and fifty miles from where I had lived on a farm. My new father was a high school teacher in Billings, so a lot of things in my life were very different from what they would have been had the flu epidemic not taken my birth parents away and consigned me to an entirely new life." I could see that what I was telling Elizabeth really interested her. I sensed her sympathetic response just by the way she looked at me. I was encouraged to go on with my story. "So the little farm kid, Karl in tiny Reese Creek, was transformed into Karl Swensen, living in a city and walking down the street to Broadwater School in Billings, the third largest city in Montana. . . ."

"That must have been quite an adjustment for you."

"I guess it might have been, but since I was never told anything about my original parents or about what happened, I really didn't know any better. . . My new parents provided for all my needs . . .almost. They had not had children of their own. . . . but. . . ."

"But what?"

"I don't know. It's just that I didn't feel the love which I now think I would have felt from my own parents. And strange to say, I don't think I ever felt that my aunt and uncle's house was home to me. I was pretty much a loner in school. I never felt that I belonged. . . I don't know why." Elizabeth gave me a sympathetic look which I'd never before felt from anyone. "This disconnected feeling stuck with me all the way through high school and Eastern Montana College in Billings." I added. "And here at the U. of C. in graduate school as well, really. . . though here it is different. People here are from all over the world. But I still felt sort of out of it." She smiled at me so warmly that I was moved to add. "Until I met you."

"I'm honored. Your honesty. I've never known a guy to be that open."

"Well, I have never really opened up to anyone like this." I felt an uneasy shyness. "It's your turn to tell me about yourself."

"Well, my family was a typical suburban family in Elmhurst. My home is a nice house on St. Charles Avenue with a big yard with lots of large elm trees. I have a brother and a sister, both of whom are away to college—Purdue in Indiana. My father is an attorney with his office in the Loop in downtown Chicago. He commutes every morning and evening on the Chicago and Northwestern. My mother is active in a lot of social things in Elmhurst. . ."

"Like what?" I wondered.

"Oh, the women's society at church—First Congregational, the local library auxiliary, and she's a member of the Elmhurst College Women's Auxiliary. . . She got involved in that during the years I went to college there."

"Wow! She's busy. . .what is your house like?"

"It is a two story with the broad side to the front, a colonial floor plan with a front door in the center with a living room to the right and a dining room on the left., a stairway up to five bed rooms on the second floor. You can see dormer windows on the second floor as you look at the front."

I had the strangest feeling while she was describing her house. I felt a slight shiver. As I think of it now I almost wonder if the house my real parents lived in perhaps might have been somewhat similar.

"As you described your house I think I began to 'see' the house of my early years before my parents died—sort of spooky."

She looked at me sympathetically. "You have so few memories of those earlier years, don't you, Karl?"

". . . just imaginary feelings I sometimes entertained when I was all alone." I could feel the beginning of a tear forming.

Elizabeth touched my hand and looked into my eyes with reciprocal sadness. "Karl, I'm sorry for the sad times you had to go through. . . and it still hurts, doesn't it?"

"It does. I'm sorry. I didn't mean to unload so much of my feeling on you, Elizabeth. After all, we have just met. . . No one else ever asked me about this stuff."

"I know, but that's just it. We seem to connect on a deeper level than we might have expected."

"Yeah—you're right."

"You must have gotten along all right in school in Billings, or else you wouldn't be here.'

"Billings had good schools and when I graduated I had a B+ average and got into Eastern where I also did pretty well."

"How did you come to go for an advanced degree here at the University of Chicago?"

"My history teacher at Eastern had gotten his degree here and he encouraged me to apply, since he saw that history was a strong subject for me. My stepparents thought it was out of my league and discouraged me. But my teacher persisted and helped me apply-- and even helped me obtain a scholarship. So here I am."

"I'm glad your teacher won that one. I was fortunate that my parents more or less assumed I would come here for a masters. This is where my parents met when they both were here as undergraduates."

"And I'm glad your parents assumed rightly." I looked at my watch and realized I needed to get to my next class. "Elizabeth, I've been going on too long about myself. I need to get to class, but thank you for listening."

"Oh, no. That's OK. Thanks for sharing with me."

I was overwhelmed by her sincerity and warmth. We parted company. "'til next time."

"For sure." This would a very special conversation I would long remember almost word for word.

CHAPTER IV

A week or so later, we were seated in a booth in a restaurant on 55th Street, not too far east of the university, waiting to order our evening meal. Elizabeth had dressed for the occasion in something a bit more "dressy" than she usually wore during the day for classes. It was a dark blue two piece suit dress with a white ruffled blouse. Similarly I wore a suit and tie.

"This is so special to be here by ourselves without the rest of the university crowd surrounding us."

"Yes." I replied. "And we won't have to get up to go to a class just when our conversation gets interesting."

There was a sort of embarrassing silence while we looked at the menu. After we ordered, Elizabeth said. "Only a couple of weeks until we have Thanksgiving break. . . I'll be glad to get home for a few days. And we will go up to our cabin at Lake Geneva for Thanksgiving dinner."

"Is that your usual family custom?"

"As long as I can remember. It's always a lot of fun. My aunt and uncle have the cabin next door and I have a couple of cousins there about my age."

"Sounds like fun." I must have sounded sad for Elizabeth immediately offered. "But, I guess that is the sort of thing you didn't have in your background?"

"No, I can't even imagine what that would be like. My stepparents didn't do much for Thanksgiving or other holidays, for that matter. And I don't remember any cousins. I remember that on Thanksgiving we sometimes went out to eat at a restaurant in downtown Billings. The Belknap Broiler, I think it was."

Elizabeth was quiet for a moment. "I'm sorry, Karl. I think you have missed out on a lot."

"Yes, I guess I did, but one tends to think only in terms of the small world you live in, and your happiness is within those limits. . ." I was a bit hesitant to go further with this, but Elizabeth had a way of opening me up. "The thing of it is that my stepmother had some sort of sect in her background in which they did not believe in celebrating anything-- birthdays, holidays, or anything else. Even though she didn't go to that church anymore some of the customs stuck with her, I guess. And my stepfather didn't seem to mind. Elizabeth, I see your world with a bit of envy, I guess."

"I see what you mean." Elizabeth was quiet and then hesitantly asked. "What will you do for the Thanksgiving weekend, Karl?"

"Hadn't thought much about it. Get more studying done. Maybe come over here for the dinner that day."

"Oh." she said with reluctance in her voice. "I have wondered, Karl. . . Have you always referred to your parents as 'stepparents'?"

"Only since I found out I was adopted."

"When was that?"

"When I was in high school, I was in a social studies class in which the subject of adoption was a topic for study. I had never thought much about adoption and certainly had not suspected anything in my case. But the more I thought abut it the more I felt I might have been adopted. The teacher said that a lot of children wonder whether they had been adopted."

"I have heard that."

"Well, after stewing about this for a number of weeks I finally got up the courage to ask my parents. We were sitting in the living room one night and I asked. 'Was I adopted?' My parents looked at each other with a sort of guilty look. "What makes you ask that?" Father asked.

"The subject of adoption came up in class, and I got to wondering."

Mother replied. "Now that you ask, I guess we had better tell you. . . yes, we adopted you after your parents died. But we didn't want you to know."

When I asked about my real parents, all they ever would say was that they had died in the flu epidemic. . . and that my mother had been my stepmother's sister."

"You never found anything else about them?"

"Just that my parents had been on a farm in Reese Creek, Montana. It still angers me that they would not tell me anything else. . .that's why I use the prefix, *step.*"This was a subject I felt uncomfortable extending any longer. I had never shared this with anyone before. It dug up some anger in me. "Tell me about Lake Geneva. Where is it? And about your cabin."

"It's north, not far into Wisconsin, maybe seventy-five miles or so. It takes Daddy a couple of hours to get there. You can go by train too. There is a little town on the edge of the lake. The rest of the lakeshore is just one summer home after another, each with its own beach and boat dock. . . ."

"Boats?"

"Mostly just row boats. . .we have two . . .they're up on land this time of the year. . . .The cabin? It is a two story frame house with two bedrooms upstairs and two down—a big living room facing the lake with wrap around porches on the lake side and the front side."

"How far is the lake from your cabin?"

"Just down the hill. . .our property goes down to the beach. . . lots of trees on the way down." Then Elizabeth added, "Aunt Gertrude's and Uncle Art's cabin next door is just like ours. We've taken the fence down so the yard and beach are twice as big."

"Do they have children?"

"Two. My cousins. . ."

"Oh, yeah, you said there were cousins next door."

". . . a girl younger than me and a boy about my age. We have always had a great time together ever since all of us were little. They are both in college at the University of Illinois in Urbana."

Our conversation about Lake Geneva ended when the waitress brought our dinners. We continued with school-related topics. "You're heading for a masters in history?" she asked me.

"Yes, U.S. History of the West, especially. . . with a minor interest in English as well You're on an English track, right?"

"Yes. American literature."

Both of us had studying to do, so when we finished dinner we left the restaurant to walk to our apartments. By this time it was dark and beginning to feel a bit chilly. Elizabeth took my arm as we walked. I felt a strange new warm closeness.

Before entering her vestibule Elizabeth slid her arm out and said. "'Karl, I enjoyed so much our dinner together. Thank you." She gave my arm a squeeze.

"I did too. See you in class."

The new found warmth continued as I walked the few blocks to my building.

On Monday Elizabeth hurried to catch up with me after class. "Karl. I talked to my folks and we would like to invite you up to the cabin for Thanksgiving! Think you could come up?"

"Why. . . sure. . . that's a surprise." I said hesitantly. "I'd like that, Elizabeth."

"Good. I'll let you know how and when to get there closer to the time."

When I got home that night all I could think about was Elizabeth and Lake Geneva. Unfortunately my pleasant anticipations were tinged with a sort of terror. A fear of being confronted by a whole batch of strangers. What would her parents think of me? How might I get on with her brother and sister, and her cousins? How could I possibly fit in? But on the other hand, I looked forward to being with Elizabeth around the clock, so to speak. . . and to meeting her mother and father. . . and to seeing the lake and the cabin.

All this uneasiness improved a little over the next days as we talked about the trip and I could get a more detailed idea of what we would do, how I would get there and what I should bring along to wear.

One nice thing that happened a week or so before Thanksgiving was a very cordial invitation which Elizabeth's mother sent me. The one line which kept coming back in my memory was. "Ellie has told us so many nice things about you, that we are all the more eager to meet you!"

When I showed that to Elizabeth she smiled demurely. I commented. "You are Ellie?"

"To my family and close friends. . . ."

"Do I qualify?"

"What do you think?"

"I hope so. . . Ellie. . . ."

"You do, Karl," she said coyly as she leaned over and kissed me on the cheek.

CHAPTER V

"**Lake Geneva**" I heard the conductor's announcement as I felt the train slowing down. I soon could see the platform in front of the depot. The steam engine was down-chugging and a flurry of smoke was swirling over the waiting crowd. We screeched to a halt amid the hissing of the pulsing boilers. I rose from my seat, grabbed my small suitcase from the overhead rack and began my walk to the front of the car. I felt a nervous excitement in anticipation of seeing Elizabeth at the station, and most likely some of her family as well. I descended the metal steps and felt the cold air as the porter helped me down onto the cement. The depot entrance was ahead of me and I walked with the crowd which had gotten off the train. Only a step or two--and there was Elizabeth hastening toward me. She quickly took my free arm and linked it to hers. "Oh, Karl, it's so exciting to see you here! Welcome to Lake Geneva!"

Thank you Ellie! I'm glad to see you too. . . even though it's only been a few days"

"I know, but here at the lake it seems so special to me."

Just then a man in a long dark overcoat and a matching fedora came up. Elizabeth turned around. "Oh, Daddy. I want you to meet Karl. . . and Karl this is my father."

"Hello, Karl. Welcome to our Wisconsin 'get-away'." Sounding quite formal, he held out his hand to me.

I responded with mine and said. "How-do-you-do, Mr, Burgess. Thank you for inviting me."

"Yes, of course. Mrs. Burgess thought it would be nice to include you at our Thanksgiving table tomorrow." I was struck by a sort of upper class tone in his voice which was new to me. "I am honored, sir."

"Well, yes. Let's go to my automobile. It's just beyond the building in the parking lot."

We soon came to a row of automobiles and Mr. Burgess pointed us to the second vehicle, a large, dark green four-door sedan with an attached trunk on the back over the bumper. I would later be informed that this was a 1929 Buick. He opened the trunk and turned to me. "You can drop your suitcase in here, and then you can sit in front with me. I can point out the sights as we drive to the cabin. And Elizabeth, you can sit in the back if you don't mind."

"Yes, Father." She sounded disappointed. I made sure to help her into her door. I took my place in the spacious passenger seat in the front. Mr. Burgess started the powerful engine and took the tall gear shift between us to move it into reverse. As we swung around and headed down one of the main business streets, I could hear the steam engine on the other side of the station as it was beginning its slow, laboring puffs to make its departure for towns further north.

Not much was said except a few times when Elizabeth's father pointed out something of interest. "That steeple over there, is our church. . . and that is the grocery store we usually use. . . and the small city library. . .and there you see the public beach." He continued to point out that sort of thing until we were out of town and turned to the left onto a narrow heavily wooded road which I assumed encircled the lake. As we drove along, I noticed that there were entry gates to one lakeside property after another. We finally came to a gate with a mail box with BURGESS printed on its side. We turned into a narrow gravel lane surrounded with trees and heavy undergrowth. Elizabeth announced excitedly, "Here we are, Karl!" I felt a wave of nervous anticipation. "Wow! Can't wait to see your place."

A cottontail rabbit scurried across the lane as we slowly made our way down toward the lake and the Burgess cabin which eventually came into view. Through trees open lighted patches appeared, which I took to be the lake.

My image of a cabin had been that of a small, two-room, one-story log hut out on a prairie, the sort of place I had seen back in Montana. What I saw in front of me as we drove up to Elizabeth's family cabin was a strikingly different scene. Before my eyes was a large two story house with a pitched roof and two dormer windows, a veritable mansion by comparison to my image of a cabin. Across the front of the house was a spacious porch, three steps up from a gravel walkway. Wicker furniture was spread around a comfortable lived-in area with a large rag rug. The entrance to the cabin was framed by large glass windows on either side on the front of the house.

Mr. Burgess brought the sedan up a short drive on the left side of the house, stopped and turned off the engine. "Here we are. Welcome to our home away from home by the lake."

"Thank you, Mr. Burgess. It looks wonderful."

Elizabeth was out of her door and rushing to open my door. She took me by the hand and led me up onto the porch. The front door opened and Elizabeth's mother pushed open a wooden screen door and hastened to greet me. Elizabeth quickly introduced me. "Mother, this is Karl–and Karl, meet my mother."

"Karl! We have been waiting to meet you, and now your are here! I'm so glad." She was all smiles. "Elizabeth has told us so much about you!"

"Thank you for inviting me for Thanksgiving."

"It's our pleasure. . . please come in." With that, she ushered me into a most inviting living room. Whereas Mr. Burgess's formality seemed cool to me, Elizabeth's mother was warm and cordial. "You're just in time for lunch. Mr. Burgess will take your suitcase up to the bedroom we have for you. Elizabeth, take Karl up and show him to his room."

And so began the first of my visits to Elizabeth's family, a new experience for me, one which I approached with a certain amount of fear and trepidation–but with a newfound happiness at being with Elizabeth for an extended time.

After a light lunch of cold cuts and cheeses along with a fruit salad, I ran up to my room, grabbed a warm jacket, and met Elizabeth waiting for me at the front door. "I want to show you the lake," she said, as she took my hand and led me across the porch and down the steps to the path leading down hill to the lakeshore. We walked out onto the Burgess pier to a bench at the far end looking out upon the lake. The afternoon sun in a nearly cloudless blue sky shone on the lake with a dazzling reflection on the gently rippling surface. The only sound was the slow lapping of the water against the posts supporting the pier. "Ellie, this I wonderful. I've never been anywhere like this."

"Karl, I just knew you would like it."

"It's so quiet and peaceful."

"I know. It's different than in the summer when everyone is here swimming, wading or in one of the boats. But times like this I like to come here and just sit. . . and think. . . ." She became serious. "Alone and away from the others."

"Oh?"

"I enjoy the family and being with the cousins and my brother and sister. We have all been here every summer since I was little. . . I guess that's part of the reason being here just with you is different. . . like when I'm alone and just thinking."

"Thinking? About what? I don't mean to be nosey, but. . . ."

"No, that's okay. Thinking? By that I mean something more like meditating, not necessarily about something in particular, but just being quiet–a chance to be myself. When I'm alone, and now with you, I can be who I am, not the little kid whom I have been here in earlier times." She seemed to stop to consider what she had said. "Don't get me wrong. I had a happy childhood. But, Karl, that's over. In some ways they all – including my parents–still see me as a child. You don't. And I like that."

"I think I see what you mean, but what is it that you think makes me see you differently, Elizabeth?"

She thought about this at some length before answering. "You see me as an equal, not some girl you look down upon, for whatever reason. . . I don't feel as though I have to play-act to impress you, or to be some sort of person who you want me to be. . . or to be afraid of you, as with some guys."

I thought about this and in comparing Elizabeth's experience to my own I observed. "I was so often alone that I didn't crave special times to be alone to think, or whatever."

Elizabeth seemed to be considering the matter further. "Then too, Karl, there is something very special for me to be looking out over the water. I feel sometimes like the water is transporting me into another world. I've never seen the ocean, but the closest thing to that for me is looking out onto Lake Michigan. You can't see the other side like you do here. . . ." She paused but was obviously engrossed in what she was telling me. "I have a favorite uncle. . . .I'm not boring you, am I?"

"Not at all."

"My mother's older brother, Roland, is someone very special for me. His earlier career was in the Merchant Marines as a sailor. He has an import business now. He never married and so in a way he sort of adopted me as his daughter. My family often visited him in his apartment on the shore of Lake Michigan, one of those tall buildings. He was on the sixteenth floor and his apartment looked out over the lake. He used to like to take me up to the window and as we looked out onto the water he would tell me about the far off places he had sailed to. But then he would also tell me how he liked to think about God and about his own life as he looked at the water–especially in the early evening when dark colored shadows seemed to paint the water in dark tints."

"That's how it began–your liking to think at the lake shore?"

"Yes, and even earlier. . . someday I'd like to have an apartment with a lake view."

"Maybe you can, Ellie. I hope so."

She paused and then became quite serious and added. "And, Karl, he was so different from my father. Father was more distant, and never spoke of God like Uncle Roland did. Not that Father does not believe in God, but it's just that he is reticent about talking about religious things."

"A lot of men are like that, I think, Ellie."

CHAPTER VI

I woke up on Thanksgiving morning, and got up to look out of my window. I could see a bright blue patch of the lake through the trees which surrounded the cabin. As I shaved and showered in a small bathroom upstairs next to my bedroom, my mind was filled with thoughts of yesterday. At supper last night and in the living room afterwards, I became acquainted with Elizabeth's sister, Dorothy and her brother David. Dorothy was talkative, reminding me of her mother, but David was more reserved and quiet like his father. I had been relieved to find them friendly to me. Surprisingly, I thought. *I could fit in, to an extent, even though our backgrounds are very different. A lot more money. . . and a social status that goes along with it. But all that doesn't seem to affect Ellie.*

My mind kept coming back to Elizabeth's sharing her fascination with the water and with her spending time thinking or meditating while gazing at the water. *That's something I've never done–don't really understand it. No such water near Billings. Maybe she'll tell me more about it. And about her uncle's sense of the divine in his life.*

When I came downstairs, I found a light breakfast buffet laid out and Elizabeth waiting for me to join her. Mrs. Burgess and her sister from next door were busy in the kitchen preparing for the Thanksgiving dinner. Before we sat down to breakfast, Ellie introduced me to her aunt. "Aunt Gertrude, I want you to meet my friend, Karl. . . and, Karl his is my aunt Gertrude."

"So good to meet you, Karl." She smiled at me and then turned to Elizabeth with a knowing smile.

"I'm glad to meet you too." Ellie and I took a few muffins, a dish
of fruit and coffee to a little table along the wall to eat our breakfast
together.

"Where is everybody?"

"Oh, Daddy–he's in his office on the phone to some client."

"Office?"

"He built a room on the side of the cabin off of the kitchen for an
office. He never quits!" Then she added to her answer, "Dorothy and
David are still asleep."

After we ate our breakfast Elizabeth announced. "I'm going to help
Mother in the kitchen. You might want to have another look down at
the shore,"

I grabbed my jacket and walked down through the tall trees to the
shore. I noticed a path which followed the shore line and went beyond
Burgess's property on both sides. I walked a little way beyond their cabin
to the next and found a similar pier, thinking this might be where Ellie's
cousins' family had their cabin. I looked forward to having Ellie share
more about their place on the lake.

After aimlessly peering out across the lake for a while, I returned
to the Burgess living room to await the festive dinner. I found some
magazines to page through until Mr. Burgess and the rest of the two
families gathered. Mr. Burgess introduced me to Ellie's cousins and to
her uncle. Soon Mrs. Burgess announced dinner and we took our places
at the table. I was glad to be seated next to Ellie.

Thanksgiving dinner was traditional in every sense of the word, as
I had always heard of it. However, it was my first such experience, in
that the usual Thanksgiving for my stepparents and me was to go to a
local restaurant in Billings.

Elizabeth sat next to me and was most solicitous in making sure
that I was comfortable with everyone around the table. There were ten
of us around the table. Mr. Burgess, at the head, carved the large turkey
and in every way presided over the proceedings. According to custom in
this family, the young people had the responsibility of doing the dishes
after the meal. This gave me a very informal chance to become better
acquainted with Ellie's brother and sister and her two cousins. By the
last dish I was feeling pretty much accepted.

By an unspoken agreement Ellie and I left the cabin to walk down
to the pier where we could talk together on our own. When I told

her that this had been my first traditional Thanksgiving dinner, she couldn't believe it

"No," I said. "Our little threesome just didn't have that kind of extended family. But I can see what a delight I have been missing. Thanks to you, my horizons are expanding, Ellie!"

"I'm glad." She didn't seem to know what more to say about that. So I could open up a conversation I had been thinking about since the day before. "Ellie, I have been wondering about your custom of thinking, or of meditation . . . ."

"What about it?"

"When did you start that sort of activity. . . or inactivity, I guess you'd say?"

Ellie took some time to formulate her answer. "When I was eight years old I got sick–very sick. The doctor said it was some sort of heart and lung condition. It hit me in the springtime and I had to stay out of school for the rest of the year. At first I was in bed most of the time. By summer I could be up; but I couldn't do anything. When it came time for us to go to the cabin the doctor said I could go to the cabin with my family if I kept from any physical activity. He thought being out-of-doors in the sunshine would probably be good for me. So we did. Daddy would be with us on the weekends and in town to go to his office during the weeks.

"When the weather was sunny and warm, mother would take me down here on the pier, bundle me up in a blanket and let me sit here while the other kids played around the water. Sometimes I got into the row boat with them"

"Wasn't that kind of dangerous, if you were to fall asleep and fall in?"

"Well, it would have been but Mom tied me to the bench with a bathrobe belt just in case. When I was in the boat, Mother held onto me tightly, but most of the time I was on the pier.'

"What did you do then? Read?"

"Sometimes, but then a lot of the time I just looked out on the lake and that's when the thinking, or meditating began."

"What sort of thoughts?"

"Oh, lots of times I'd imagine myself being on a ship out to sea sailing to some far off land. But it was Uncle Roland who introduced me to what he called God thoughts. He liked to quote from the creation story in the Bible–*And the Spirit of God was moving over the face of the waters*–which he explained gave him God thoughts when he looked out over the waters."

"And he helped you to think such thoughts?"

"The summer I was sick, Uncle Roland came out to the cabin to see me, and that's when he shared this exercise in meditation with me. I was too young at the time to really understand, but as I got older I found his idea appealing to me and now I think that way sometimes."

"Did you get over your sickness?"

"It took me three weeks into the summer, but I got better. But had to be careful for a while because they said that my condition could lead to heart problems later on. But fortunately that didn't happen. . . so far at least."

On the next two days Elizabeth showed me around the lake near their cabin. Elizabeth's mother drove us into town to do some souvenir shopping. On Sunday morning, I went to church with the family. First Congregational Church in Lake Geneva was their church during the summers and whenever they were at the cabin.

After Sunday dinner at the cabin, Mr. Burgess took Elizabeth and me into town to catch the train for Chicago. The rest of the family returned home to Elmhurst in the family Buick.

Elizabeth and I transferred to a streetcar which took us to Hyde Park. We walked to her apartment building. When we came to her door we took each other's hands. "Ellie, this has been one of the best times in my life. It was so good to be with you and your family. . . to feel vicariously what home must be like for you. Thank you so very much."

"Oh, Karl. I'm so glad you were with me at the cabin. I can't wait to have you there in the summer when we can enjoy swimming and boating together. Thank you for coming with me."

With that we looked into each other's eyes and I drew her to me and we kissed good bye!. . . until tomorrow.

CHAPTER VII

When we returned to our school routine we found more and more ways of spending time with each other. We arranged it so that we could eat all of our lunches together at Hutchison. On the weekends we studied together in the library and often went out for supper at one of the nearby restaurants. Sunday mornings we went to church together and to dinner afterward.

One evening I received a surprise phone call. "Hello, Karl Swensen here."

"Hello, this is Roland Whitaker, Elizabeth Burgess's uncle,"

"Yes, Mr. Whitaker. Elizabeth has mentioned you frequently."

"And I have heard some good things about you from Elizabeth's family. I would like to meet you, Karl. Might I take you to lunch some day?"

"I'd enjoy meeting you, and lunch sounds good to me."

"Then may we meet down in the Loop at the Union League Club at one o'clock this next Thursday?"

"That would be fine, sir."

"Good. I'll meet you at the reception desk at one o'clock. Do you know where the Union League Club is?"

"Not really, but I'll look it up."

"No, let me give you directions." He told me exactly how to get there.

Later that day when I was with Elizabeth, I told her about the phone call. "Your uncle Roland phoned me and wants to take me to lunch on Thursday."

"That's nice. I wonder what he has in mind."

"I wonder too. Except to get acquainted, as he said."

"I think you will really like him, Karl."

On Thursday I made my way to the Loop and found the Union League Club on Jackson just as Uncle Roland had explained. I went in to the desk and found Roland waiting for me. "Karl, I believe. I'm Roland Whitaker."

"How do you do sir. I'm Karl Swensen."

"Yes Let's go in to our luncheon."

We were met at the door to the dining room by the Maitre d'. "Hello, Mr. Whitaker. I have your usual table ready, sir." He then led us to a table for two at one of the windows, and gave us leather-bound menus. When we were seated Roland put down his menu and suggested. "I think chicken cordon bleu would be good, don't you?"

"Yes, that would be fine."

"And a pot of tea?"

"Good."

A waiter appeared and took our order.

While this ordering process was going on, I had a chance to observe Roland Whitaker. A slender man neatly dressed in a three-piece gray suit with a white shirt and a blue polka dot bow tie. A gentle curl in his speckled gray hair and a matching trimmed mustache. There was a warm expression in his soft brown eyes.

"I understand you are from Montana. Whereabouts?"

"Originally from Gallatin County near Bozeman, and then later from Billings."

"I haven't been to Bozeman or Billings, but I have been in Butte. Had some business there."

"What sort of business are you in."

"The import business. I was in the Merchant Marine for many years and when I got out, the import business was a natural for me. I love traipsing around the globe making business contacts in other countries and I love sailing on the ocean blue! Everyone thinks I should live on of one of the coasts. But there are all sorts of importers there. In Chicago I can get a better share of the market, don't you know?"

"I see what you mean."

"Now, tell me about Billings. That's where you grew up, I take it?"

"Yes, since I was five years old when I was moved into my aunt and uncle's house in Billings. . ."

"House? That's a strange way to put it."

"Well, what happened was that my parents died in the flu epidemic of '18. Before I knew what was going on, I was living with my aunt and uncle in their house. They adopted me."

"I see. . . ."

It didn't seem to me that he understood fully. "They were–and are--both school teachers. Which, I guess, is why I plan to teach when I get my degree."

"You plan to teach in Montana?"

"That's what I had planned, but now that I am at the University of Chicago I guess I am thinking more in terms of teaching in college somewhere in this area."

"Sounds good. What subject?"

"History."

"Before you moved to Billings, where were you?"

"My birth parents lived in Reese Creek, near Bozeman."

"You don't have any memories of that time?'

"Hardly, and I never have learned much about my parents except that they died in the influenza epidemic in 1918. I have no knowledge of my true heritage, but I wish I could find out more about my blood roots."

"Yes, and I think you should. I bellieve it helps a person to find oneself, if one knows about how ones heritage has shaped one. Your adoptive parents didn't tell you much about that?"

"No, they were very closed mouth about my background."

"My advice to you, Karl, is that you ask them to give you as much information as they have."

"I guess you have something there for me to consider. . . ."

The waiter brought our meals which had the effect of bringing this discussion to a turning point. "Let's enjoy our lunch before continuing our thoughts."

Eventually Roland put down his knife and fork. "After a bit we can have some dessert." He turned to me and said. "I thought I might give you a bit of history concerning Elizabeth. To begin with, I have always been quite close to my sister, Elizabeth's mother. And ever since Elizabeth was born, I have had a soft spot in my heart for her. Especially since I never married and do not have children of my own. So, ever since becoming aware of her growing relationship with you, Karl, I have wanted to include you also as a friend of mine. As perhaps you are aware, I have shared with Elizabeth my special love of the sea, of the water. I have enjoyed their family cabin on Lake Geneva and have shared with Elizabeth my view of Lake Michigan from my apartment on the north side."

"Yes, she told me of your meditative use of the water. Something quite new to me, coming from Montana. . . although I think folk out there sometimes find the mountains to be a similar experience for them, especially serious mountain climbers."

"Yes I think that is so. When I was in Nepal, I came in contact with some serious mountain climbers who had tackled Everest. Some of them spoke of their ascent as a spiritual experience. Anyway, it was at the time of Elizabeth's illness that we connected with each other in this way. She has told you about her illness?"

"Yes."

"When she was so sick, I helped her through it by showing her how I gained inspiration gazing out across the waters. An old seaman had taught me this, and it helped me a lot especially at lonely times in my life at sea."

The waiter brought our desserts. We took time out of our conversation, which we resumed over coffee. Roland announced, "After the first of the year, I have an overseas trip to do some buying and I've asked Elizabeth if she would spend her nights in my apartment during that time. There are some housekeeping things I need doing like watering my plants; and I just feel safer having someone there while I am gone. Public transportation is convenient between my place and Hyde Park." He took out his watch from his vest pocket. " I have an appointment at the office and need to let you go, Karl. But I have appreciated getting to know you. I'm sure we will have other opportunities to get together."

"Certainly, and I do appreciate the fine luncheon you have treated me to, Mr. Whitaker."

"A pleasure. Call me Uncle Roland, by the way."

With that we rose and he escorted me to the street where we parted.

I met Ellie later that afternoon after her last class. She asked me. "Did you pass?" At first I didn't know what she was referring to. Then I realized she was wondering about what her uncle thought of me. " Oh, that! Yes, with flying colors, I think."

"I'm so glad. That means a lot to me."

"He told me about asking you to stay in his apartment in January. Do you plan to?"

"I haven't said. Truth is, I wanted to ask you what you thought."

"If you want to, Ellie. We can work around that, I'm sure."

"I think I do want to. Sounds sort of fun. . . .but before that it will be Christmas. Will you be here over the holidays?"

"No, I'm sorry to say, but my stepparents wish I could come to see them, and I think I had better do that."

"Maybe you and I could do a little celebrating before you leave, Karl."

"I'd like that. What did you have in mind?"

"One thing I used to do with my parents each year, we could do – just you and I."

"What's that?"

Elizabeth explained to me the way they used to spend a day in the Loop visiting Marshall Fields before Christmas and we agreed that we would do that on a day or two after we were off school for the holidays.

Two weeks remained during which we both were super busy with school work and exams. When I had more time to myself after exams, I kept coming back to Uncle Roland's advice about asking my stepparents more about my background.'

I made arrangements with the Northern Pacific Railroad for a coach seat to Billings on December 20th.

CHAPTER VIII

After classes on December 15th, I returned to my apartment and picked up my mail on the way into my building. There was an official looking envelope from Bozeman with a return address of a local law firm. When I opened it, I was shocked to find the following letter:

Dear Mr. Swensen:

This is to advise you of a bequest which had been made to you for your rightful claim at the age of your maturity. We have not been able to locate you until recently. We have just lately obtained your new name after your adoption and your current address, Although your age of majority will not been reached for another four years we would like to meet you so that we can discuss this bequest. Please notify us of your receipt of this letter and we can then arrange to have you come to our office so that we can inform of the details of your late parents' will.

Yours respectfully,
A.B. Sutherland

I replied, saying that I would be in Montana after December 21 and that I would contact the law firm for an appointment at that time. I couldn't wait to tell Ellie, and when I did, she immediately asked me excitedly. "Do you have any idea what this is about?"

"No, I can't imagine. I guess I will have to wait until I see the lawyer and he reads me the will. As soon as I get to Montana, I'll make a trip to

Bozeman and see the law firm. Until then I just need to put the whole thing on the back burner so that we can have a bit of Christmas with each other, Ellie."

We both made it through our tests and finally the Christmas break came and we arranged for the special day which Ellie had promised. And then the following day I would leave for Montana and to find out what the lawyer had for me. And I would have a few days over Christmas to spend with my step parents.

Mr. Swensen put his pen down and closed his notebook. It was time to return to the present and to his responsibilities as a professor at Elmhurst College.

Elmhurst 1948

The Northwestern pulled into the station at Elmhurst Sunday afternoon. The short ride on the train as usual gave him a transition period in which he left his thoughts of his "other life," as he came to call it, and to return to his current life as a professor of history at Elmhurst College. This was the beginning of his fifteenth year of teaching at the college which he had come to love. It was a college with a small enrollment. Although with the return of World War II veterans, its student body had recently grown considerably.

Elmhurst, itself, was a beautiful modest sized suburb west of Chicago. York Street, its main north-south street, and Prospect Street were known for being fully arched over with tall elm trees along each side of the street. The college was on Prospect Street a block west of York. Now, as Mr. Swensen walked under the elms, he saw that they were just starting to turn color on this early October late afternoon. The opening lines of the Alma Mater rang through his consciousness. *Where the elms in stately glory spreading branches raise. . . .*

Many of the faculty lived in college housing along the north side of the campus, not far from the president's house on Prospect. As a single man, Karl Swensen occupied two adjoining rooms, one for his office and the other for his personal apartment, on the third floor of the administration and classroom building, known as Old Main. Most of the student body lived on campus and took their meals in the Commons.

Near the Commons was Old Main in which Mr. Swensen taught his classes. The college library was across from Old Main. Just west was South Hall, the women's dormitory. On the north side of the campus was Irion Hall, the men's dorm which also housed the music department and the chapel.

Mr. Swensen walked the few blocks from the train depot to the campus. He went up to his room. An hour or so later he came down stairs for supper in the Commons. After loading his tray he walked past Dale Schmidt and Maynard Otterberg, students in one of his classes, on his way to a place for himself. They greeted him as he passed and found his usual place toward the back of the dining hall away from the crowded tables.

"Must be Sunday night. Mr. Swensen is back from his weekend," Dale commented to Maynard.

"Just like clockwork. Tomorrow morning at eight we'll be in class with him," Maynard replied. "Why don't you see him before class for your question?"

"Yeah, I'll do that."

The next morning they went to class in Old Main. They arrived early enough for Dale to see Mr. Swensen before class. He obtained the answer he needed.

Their Monday morning class was "Frontiers in the West," an advanced history course in which Maynard and Dale were enrolled as juniors. The basis for ths course was a book which Karl Swensen had published a few years earlier. *MONTANA'S SIX FRONTIERS*. While the book was not used as a text book, its table of contents provided the broad outline of the course.

SIX FRONTIERS IN THE HISTORY OF THE AMERICAN WEST
1. Fur Frontier-1804-Lewis and Clark, Mountain men -1864
2. Mining Frontier-1858-Gold, Silver, Copper Coal-ongoing
3. Livestock Frontier-1850s- Open Range Land and Cattle companies- 1900
4. Agricultural Frontier-1900-Homesteading, Agricultural Extension.
5. Petroleum Frontier-1915-Oil, Gas extraction, Refineries

6.   Tourism-recreation Frontier-Hunting, Fishing, Dude ranching, National Parks.

Toward the end of the class hour, Mr. Swensen announced, "I am planning to conduct a session scheduled for the first week after the end of Spring Semester. It is to be held in a small study center in Gallatin County, Montana, near Bozeman. Those completing the field course will receive three hours credit. We will focus on the six frontiers as covered in this course and we will have on-site visits pertaining to each of the frontiers. These will be located in Montana and northern Wyoming. The costs of this experience for up to fifteen participants will be covered substantially from a grant which I have obtained. In succeeding weeks I will have more specific arrangements for the field study. Those interested, need to make a commitment for this event by January 15th."

The bell rang, signaling the end of class. As the students filed out, Mr. Swensen distributed flyers regarding the field study. There was a great deal of excitement over the prospects of the field study, as everyone was leaving class.

That night Dale and Maynard poured over the field study announcement. "This sounds like something I would really like to do." Dale declared.

"Me too. I've never been west of the Mississippi and this would be great. It would be fun if both of us could go."

"Yeah. Then maybe we'll get to know Swensen a bit more. There really is a mystery about him. He lives alone and doesn't seem to have friends. . . and then those weekend departures. What's that about?"

"Maybe he's got a lady friend somewhere. . . ."

"Doubt it. . . not the type."

"Oh well. I like the idea of the field study, regardless." The two friends talked about this possibility long into the evening. They decided that they would sign up for this field study, if they could work the schedule into their summer plans.

CHAPTER IX

Only a week remained before the Christmas break, when everyone would head home for the holiday season. Maynard would go home to St. Louis and Dale to eastern Iowa. One of the usual celebrations on campus was scheduled for the last Saturday of the term. It was a special dinner in the Commons after which students formed caroling groups which went out into the community visiting various places in town.

Mr. Swensen used his entire Saturday for reading student papers and grading tests so that he could leave campus without any work hanging over his head. He was eager to get back to writing his story.

He took an early Sunday morning train from Elmhurst and arrived in the city in time to attend worship at Fourth Presbyterian Church on Michigan Boulevard, north of the Loop on what is called "The Magnificent Mile." After the 11:00 clock service, he stopped in a café for a quick lunch and then went up to his Lake Shore apartment. He would now have the better part of two weeks in which to continue, if not complete, his story.

Once again Mr. Swensen writes more of
his earlier story of 17 ears ago

Chicago – December 1931

On our first free day of Christmas break I met Ellie at her apartment for our Christmas trip. My first surprise of the day was to see what an attractive navy blue suit she had chosen to wear with a deep red silk blouse and moderately high heels. We took the "L" train into the Loop, getting off at State and Dearborn. We then went to Marshall Fields.

"Just wait 'til you see the Christmas decorated windows!" Ellie exclaimed, as we approached the corner.

"Wow, look at that!" I said as I came up to a series of six windows, three on each side of the corner of the building with the iconic clock overhanging the corner sidewalk. Each window had an elaborate Christmas scene, most of which featured toys of one kind or another, many of which were moving as we gazed in wonder. Electric trains passed by in one of the windows. Some gaily dressed dolls were in another and stuffed animals rocked back and forth in other windows.

"You were right, Ellie. I am amazed. Never have seen anything close to this." I thought of Billings at Christmas. "Nothing in Montana, nearly this ornate."

"Now, I want you to see the beautiful decorations inside. . . especially the huge Christmas tree in the center atrium."

Inside the department store I was amazed all over again with aisle after aisle of upscale and fashionable merchandise tastefully on display. The pillars along each aisle were festooned with pine bows bristling with huge silver balls. Even the clerks looked as though they had just stepped out of a very fancy fashion magazine, to say nothing of the fact that the customers also looked as though they had just come out of a high level board meeting somewhere. I felt as though I had not dressed up enough to be seen in such a place as this.

Ellie and I went up the escalator to see the tree in the atrium from above. The escalator was a new experience for me as I carefully stepped onto the moving tread. As we passed each floor we were surrounded by elegant decorations and counter tops filled with colorful arrays of things to purchase. Ellie led the way off one of the upper floors, where we could step over to a railing and look down upon the magnificently decorated Christmas tree filling the atrium. She led me into a most impressive restaurant trimmed in polished dark wood, appropriately called the Walnut Room. A formally dressed hostess ushered us to a table for two and gave each of us a menu encased in a leather cover. Ellie suggested a chicken salad plate with hot tea, after which we were served a cherry torte for desert. Again I felt out of place as I looked around at a room full of finely dressed patrons and found myself wishing we were comfortably back in Hutchison cafeteria, if not in a local café in Billings. Places where I belonged.

We talked of the holidays and about what each would be doing. Ellie told about a regular get-together she and some of her high school girl friends had each year the week before Christmas. And she shared a bit about the traditions which were experienced in her home in the family. When she asked me about my memories I had to say, "Not much." Sensing my discomfort with this answer, she asked me about my forthcoming trip to the lawyer.

"Have you thought anything more about the will which he is going to read, Karl?"

"No, I can't think what that is about. Everything was settled, I thought, after my parents died. And then when I was adopted, they would have been the only persons involved in such matters."

"I guess you are right."

"Oh well, in a few days, I'll see what's what."

At that we got up and made our way out of the Walnut Room and to the escalators to take them down to the street.

On our way back to Hyde Park on the "L," we sat very close and held hands. Ellie was strangely quiet and seemed somewhat sad. I ventured to ask. "Why are you sad?'

"Oh, I wish you could be with me in our home for Christmas. We have gotten to enjoy each other's company, and I am going to miss that."

"So will I. I feel as if I am going back to another world. . . a world more familiar to me and at the same time so different from to the world here in Chicago--a world with you, Ellie"

A quiet pall descended until Ellie broke the silence with, "In the week after Christmas my brother and sister and I usually have an at-home party for all our friends. . . I sure wish you could be here for that, Karl. Do you suppose you could?"

"When is it?"

"On December 30th, usually."

"I could take the train back on the 29th."

"That would be great."

As we got closer to Hyde Park we exchanged information about when each would leave Hyde Park for home.

"My train to Montana is tomorrow. I am going all the way to Bozeman so that I can see the attorney. My stepfather will drive to

Bozeman and meet me after I have been to see the attorney. Then he'll take me back to Billings. So, I'll take the "L" to the station tomorrow morning."

"Daddy is coming for me the day after tomorrow."

When we got to Ellie's apartment door we kissed "good bye."

"Merry Christmas, Ellie."

"Merry Christmas, Karl."

The next morning I boarded the Northern Pacific for Bozeman. The lengthy train ride alone gave me lots of time to think During my trip home, my thinking bounced back and forth from my schooling and the career for which I was preparing. *A few more months at U. of C. And I should be finding a teaching job in a college somewhere. Ever since I was in early years of high school I have dreamed of being a college prof. I can see that this is a reasonable hope after making my way in my university courses. As Elizabeth has come into my life, it appears to me that this goes along with my career dreams. Her hopes are similar to mine, I think, although we haven't talked about this very much. We ought to. But, then when I am honest, I think about how different her economic and social background is from mine. Sometimes I think that doesn't matter, then other times I know that is a problem. Now I am on a track going from Ellie's world to my world. . . or is it still my world? I wonder, was it ever?*

Pillows were handed out after the train left St. Paul and night shadows were falling. I found that I could sleep fairly well as the coach sped along the rails. When we passed through towns, the crossing bells often awakened me and I watched the lamp posts slip by. When I awakened to sunlight I found that the train was in Montana.

It was then that my thoughts began to focus on learning more about my heritage and about what I would be hearing from the attorney in Bozeman. I didn't have a clue, since my only memories were mostly from life in Billings. Once again I found myself disturbed at my lack of information about my origins, except that I had lived with my birth parents in Reese Creek until I was five years old. I wondered what an attorney in Bozeman have to do with my life?

My reverie was halted by the announcement of the approaching stop at Bozeman. *I'll soon find out what's up,* I thought as I collected my overhead luggage and prepared to step onto the platform. As the train rolled to a stop, I saw that the entire landscape was covered with a fairly thick accumulation of snow. I entered the depot and walked though to the street side and found what I later was told was Bozeman's only taxi cab. It was waiting to pick up a few arrivals needing transportation. I gave the driver the address of the attorney on East Main Street. After two others got into the cab, it left for Main Street. It surprised me how far away from Main the train station was located. It was also impressive to see snow covered mountains so near to town. After paying the cab driver, I walked over to the door with the attorney's name on it in black-lined gold letters. The door led immediately to a stairway to the second floor where I stepped up to the reception desk. "I am here to see Mr. Sutherland. I am Karl Swensen."

CHAPTER X

The meeting with the attorney, Mr. Sutherland, took place in a conference room above Security Bank on Bozeman's Main Street. A representative of the bank also attended this meeting. When all were seated the attorney addressed me.

"Mr. Swensen, we have determined that the name given at your birth was *Karl Lars Erickson* and that at the age of five you were adopted and given the name of your adoptive parents. Thus, your legal name is now *Karl Lars Swensen*.

"Now, in your birth parents' will at the time of their death, their real property at Reese Creek, Montana, in Gallatin County was to be left to you at the time of your majority, and in the mean time to be held in trust by First Security Bank of Bozeman."

The attorney then read the will, which simply put what the lawyer had already spelled out. He then continued. "By the time you turn twenty-one, you will have been adopted by Mr. & Mrs. Swensen. This was not known at the time to us or to the bank. There was apparently some confusion in the record keeping by the county. For most of the intervening years the bank rented the farm out, but for the last number of years the property has been unoccupied. Contrary to the assumptions of the bank, the renter chose not to occupy the house and remained in their own house nearby in Reese Creek, and the bank has carried out almost no maintenance, assuming you would be soon found. Thus the condition of the house has deteriorated considerably. This brings us to the present."

"Before I continue, are there any questions?"

I replied. "Before I have any questions, I need to tell you that since I did not know I had been adopted until I was in high school, and then no further information was given me, I had no idea I had another name at birth."

The attorney showed surprise. "I see! Then you have been in the dark as the bank has."

I then asked. "During this time how have the expenses and the rental income been cared for by the bank?"

The banker responded. "A special account has been set up from which all expenses, such as taxes, have been paid, and the rental income has been held in that account. We shall of course give a complete statement and the balance will be turned over to the total assets of the property to be presented to you, Mr. Eric. . . Swensen when you reach age twenty-one.

"In the next intervening four years we will keep in touch with you, Mr. Swensen. Thank you very much for coming in today. It helps us greatly to have proper contact with you while this property remains in our trust on your behalf.

When I left the office I stopped at the reception desk to use her phone to contact my stepfather. Our arrangement was that after my meeting with the attorney, I would phone him at the Bozeman Hotel where he will have booked a room. "Hello, this is Karl. I will be at the café on the north side of Main Street about a block east of Security Bank. Can you meet me there in about twenty minutes?. . . Good. I'll see you in twenty minutes."

I was overwhelmed in more ways than one as I left the attorney's office. However, I needed some time to process this unheard-of information before meeting my stepfather. I remembered the cab passing by a café on Main street a block or two before we reached my destination. I walked east along Main until I found the café and entered it. I took a seat at a table for two and ordered some coffee and a sweet roll. I simply could hardly believe what the attorney told me. I had no idea about any of that. Did my stepparents know anything about all this? My mind raced through a jumble of questions.

Where's the property? What shape is it in? What is it like? What about the farm? Who's farming it? What's it all worth? Did my stepparents know anything about this and why did I never know about it?

At this point my anger surfaced. *I need to get some answers.* I looked up to see my stepfather entering the café. I motioned to him and he came to the table. After greeting each other, he joined me at the table. "What was the attorney visit all about, Karl?"

"He informed me of an inheritance which shall be mine when I reach twenty one."

"An inheritance?"

"Yes. . . Tell me what you knew of my birth parents and their house and their farm. No more excuses to keep me from knowing anything about my background." I said in anger.

He took a long moment to formulate his answer. "To begin with, your birth mother, Anna Erickson, was your mother's sister. I was under the impression that the farm had been rented by your parents. Your father was always tight mouthed about financial matters. We didn't think your mother knew much about such things either. In fact, your father and I were not close. . .to say the least. . . so far as our not sharing anything with you, I can only say that we had been so sorry not to have been able to have children, that when we took you, we wanted you to be ours only. . .and that led us to be closed mouth about your background. And I can see that we probably should have been more forthcoming with you. I am sorry."

"I wish you had shared with me what you knew of my background."

"So far as your background is concerned, we didn't know much about your father's ancestry, and very little about your mother's and my wife's ancestry.

"Well, certainly as a little kid, I didn't have the slightest idea. So that today when the attorney told me of my inheritance, I was completely taken aback."

"Yes, I am very sorry. . . Can you tell me what you heard from the attorney?"

I then told him about the inheritance. "And I don't have any idea what I should do now."

My stepfather offered his idea. "I think you need to see the place and get some idea of what shape it is in. And it seems to me that, unless you plan to become a farmer, you will want to sell the farm. And you are going to have to get an idea of what the buildings need in order to be saleable."

"That means we ought to line up a realtor now even though it is a few years before it is mine, to help me to assess the situation."

"If we stay overnight, I think we could go out tomorrow with a realtor before going home to Billings."

"I agree."

The next morning we arranged with a local realtor to go out to Reese Creek with us to examine what it is that I will inherit. Fortunately, there was less snow in this area than in town. When we pulled into the farm, I had a very dim memory of what I was seeing. But I was appalled to see how the house had fallen into decay. Fortunately, the metal roof was in good shape so that the interior was saved from leakage. However the doors and windows were gone. Apparently and surprisingly the structure appeared to be sound. The barn and one of the sheds had completely collapsed, which I learned later had been the result of the 1925 earthquake. The smaller sheds appeared to be in fair condition. One old log cabin caught my eye. Apparently it had been the first residence of those who must have homesteaded here.

The farm faced west. Not very far to the east was a mountain range. Directly behind the farm rose a rocky peak. The realtor told us that this was the Bridger Range and the prominent mountain was Ross Peak.

The realtor had brought a camera with him and took some snapshots of the house and out buildings. After looking things over, the realtor said. "If the house were to be completely renovated and the yard and outbuildings cleaned up, I think we could put the farm on the market and get a pretty good price."

"Can you give me a figure?" I asked. "In today's depression market."

"I'll need to get back to the office and work that out for you, including renovation costs. I have a friend in the building contracting business who can help me determine that. I should be able to let you know in a week so." He added as a caution. "But by the time it is yours the depression figures won't pertain."

"I realize that. . . . We will be back in Billings by the time you have the estimates, I assume."

"I can mail you my estimates."

"Let me give you my permanent address in Chicago. That would be a better place to send information in the future."

After our conference with the realtor, we drove to Billings. I resolved to put the farm business out of my mind so that I could enjoy Christmas with my stepparents. The very open and honest exchange with my stepfather in the café, and also when we went out to the farm, had the effect of removing much of the anger which I had felt about my relationship with my stepparents over the question of the my background. However, there remained the complete blackout concerning my birth-parents. I needed to hear much more about my birth family from my stepparents, or possibly from others in the Reese Creek community who had known them.

We went to church on Christmas Eve. The next morning we gathered around the tree in the living room and exchanged gifts. It was a relaxing celebration in which I felt more at ease in the family setting in which I had grown up than I had anticipated

On Christmas afternoon, we went to the Custer Hotel dining room for a traditional baked ham dinner. That night we drove around the residential areas of Billings to look at decoration lights put up for the season. I felt eons away from my life in Chicago. Thoughts of Elizabeth intruded from time to time but always with a sense of separation. That bothered me and made me want to return to Chicago, even though another part of me wanted to remain in Montana, to learn more of my background.

The letter from the realtor came to the Billing address instead of Chicago the day after Christmas giving me a ballpark estimated cost of renovating the house and cleaning up the yard and outbuildings. A large enough figure to scare me. But the price he preliminarily put on the farm was higher than I had imagined, so that if I could sell the farm at that price and pay for the renovation it seemed to me that I would come out pretty well. All this would work out if I could get a loan on the property to cover renovation costs. A big IF. Especially when one considers that the figures given me now were be affected by the Depression.

Apparently the banker had mentioned to the realtor my having been completely cut off from my birth parents. This prompted him to mention in his letter to me that he had recently sold a house in Billings to a couple who had lived in Reese Creek some years ago. He gave me their phone number in case I wanted to contact them.

I would not be in Montana long enough at this time to make any preliminary decisions or to work out any plans for he future. I discussed all this with my stepfather, and he was quite interested in helping with the project when it would take place after the property would become mine.

At this point my thinking was to sell the property and to invest the funds which remained after all the expenses had been cared for.

I spent the remaining days in Billings visiting with my parents and doing things with them like "old times." I thought of Ellie on and off, but she seemed so far away and living in a separate world. My train reservation was for December 29 and I would arrive in Chicago on the 30th in time for the "at home" party she was having that evening in Elmhurst. . . which I did not look forward to very happily. I know it was my innate shyness, but it also had to do with wondering what sort of "high class" friends of hers I would be meeting.

I phoned Mr. and Mrs. Ferguson, of whom my realtor spoke. "Hello, Mrs. Ferguson. I am Karl Swensen. I'm told you used to live in Reese Creek, over in Gallatin County."

"Yes we did. How can I help you?"

"My parents were Jon and Anna Erickson. . . . ""

"Oh my, I knew them well, but of course after they both died in the flu epidemic, I lost track of the family."

"I can see that. . . I was adopted immediately by my mother's sister in Billings, so I too lost complete track of Reese Creek until recently. I'd like to know more about my parents. Might I come to see you?"

"Of course. We would like to meet you."

We made arrangements for me to visit the next evening.

The Fergusons cordially welcomed me into their living room. When we were settled in easy chairs and went through preliminary introductions, Mrs. Ferguson eagerly began to tell me about my mother and how they had been good friends and neighbors in the Reese Creek community.

"In 1912 we joined the Montana Equal Suffrage Association and attended some rallies in Helena on that issue. Miss Jeanette Rankin, who later became the first woman U.S. Senator, was very active in this women's crusade. A couple of years later we managed to get the women's vote through the state legislature. Your mother and I were ecstatic. Then in the year or two following, we were again rallying, this time to promote Jeanette Rankin's candidacy for the Senate."

I listened with rapt attention. "My mother did all that! On top of being a farm wife?"

"Yes, we all did, and in April of 1917 Miss Rankin took her seat as a senator from Montana—the first woman from any state!"

"Wow! Did my father go along with her activism?"

"He did. I think he was quite proud of her."

Mr. Ferguson chimed in. "Yes, we both were proud of our wives. . ." But then he turned sorrowful. "But a little over a year afterward your mother died of the flu—your father as well."

"And so many others." Mrs. Ferguson added sadly.

I then said. "I was only five years old. And I don't remember any of that. My aunt came immediately and took me from the house to keep me from the disease and the next thing I knew I was growing up in Billings. And what you have told me tonight is the first information I have ever gotten about my parents."

The Fergusons looked shocked to hear this.

"I really appreciate what you have shared with me. More than you can ever know. . . but I must go now. I'll want to keep in touch, however."

"Certainly, Karl. It has been our pleasure to re-connect with your family,"

As the time for my departure to Chicago drew near, I asked my stepparents to sit down with me and share with me all that they knew about my birth parents.

When we all sat down in the living room around the Christmas tree the tension in the room was palpable. After a substantial silence my stepmother began. My stepfather added things from time to time as my story came out for the first time in my life.

"Well, to begin with your mother was my sister, Anna, who was two years older than I was. We grew up in Minneapolis. We both went to normal school to obtain teaching degrees. We both eventually came to Montana to find teaching jobs. I found a job in Shepherd and after a couple of years got a position in Billings where I met Albert and we married. Anna was hired in a little one room school in Reese Creek. She boarded on one of the farm homes in the community, the Ericksons. Well, eventually she married one of the Erickson sons, Jon, who remained on the farm and finally took it over from his father. Jon and Anna had a baby in due time, whom they named, Karl.

"When you were five years old, the influenza epidemic hit. Both your parents died of it. Though we had not remained close, your mother contacted me when she was coming down with the flu and asked if I would take you in the event that both she and Jon died. We agreed. In fact both of us were delighted at the possibility since we had wanted children and had not been able to have any. We came over to get you in order to keep you from catching the flu. When the Gallatin County health department notified us of your parents' death, we immediately came to care for funeral arrangements. We were so happy to have you, that we decided then and there never to mention anything to you about the tragedy of your parents' deaths."

It would be awhile for me to process what I had just heard but I thanked my stepparents and determined in my own mind to rebuild an adult relationship with them. . . which would come in time, to some extent.

CHAPTER XI

As my train carried me back to Chicago, I spent a considerable amount of time wondering about the Erickson farm and its heritage as exemplified in the little log cabin in Reese Creek, which would be mine, as well as the later buildings along with the farm land.

I returned to my apartment in Hyde Park for an overnight before going out to Elmhurst to meet Ellie. In the midst of my former surroundings at the university, I sensed a strange feeling of dislocation. . . as if I were a different person from when I had last been in Chicago. Somehow the sudden discovery of who my real parents had been and where I had lived had been a jolt. This in some way made me question who I had been all these years since my adoption. Tiny fragments of memory had come to mind–the faces of my mother and father-- sounds and smells of the farm–and of the house–the mountains east of Reese Creek. At the same time, images of my stepparents seemed to be receding. And now it seemed strange to be here in my Chicago apartment and involved in the University of Chicago.

The next morning I returned to the Loop and boarded the Northwestern for Elmhurst and Ellie's at-home party. This would be my first visit to Elmhurst and to her home. I was eager to see her, but at the same time I was apprehensive. I had already been shaken up with my identity shift. How would Ellie appear to me now? What were her friends like?

She was waiting in the depot when my train pulled into the station. Embarrassed, we greeted each other warmly. As she led me through the station to the street, she explained. "My friend from next door offered to give us a ride home." We reached his car and he got out. "Karl, this is Dick Campbell, my neighbor. Dick, this is Karl."

"Good to meet you, Dick," I said as we shook hands.

"Hello, Karl," he replied as he ushered me into the front passenger seat of his new Oldsmobile. "Welcome to Elmhurst."

"Thank you. It's beautiful. I've never seen such a lot of tall trees like these over the street."

Ellie chimed in. "Yes. Elms. This is Prospect Street. You can see why it is called 'Elmhurst'"

I felt an embarrassing silence for the few more blocks it took Dick to get to the Burgess house, where Ellie announced. "This is home!"

As I saw the house, I again had that wistful feeling of seeing the house at Reese Creek in its better days. Dick drove into the driveway briefly to let us off. Ellie thanked him and said, "We will see you later on at the party." I thanked him, which he acknowledged.

Ellie eagerly led me up to the front door where her mother greeted me enthusiastically. I stepped into a magnificent foyer with a highly polished stairway ahead of me and sparkling glazed doors on my right and left, leading to a formal dining room on one side and an elegant living room on the other.

"Elizabeth, you can show Karl to his room. He probably wants to freshen up before the big party. And then, I need your help in the kitchen."

"Sure, Mom."

I went up the center stairs following Ellie and into the room she pointed out. "This used to be my room when I was little. And now, it's so much fun having you here, Karl."

"Thank you, Ellie." I said as she showed me into a richly furnished bedroom decorated in powder pink with white trim.

"Come down to the living room when you are ready and we can visit a bit before everyone shows up."

"Good. I'll be down later." After entering the bedroom and closing its door behind me, I felt overwhelmed in this large, richly appointed home. Any comparison with the house on Reese Creek faded away completely. I clearly felt out of place here, and in some sense dreaded going downstairs to join Ellie and her family. I felt even more ill at ease as I contemplated the party later in the evening. I wished I were back in Hutchison sitting alone with my supper tray. When I heard Mrs.

Burgess call to me that dinner was ready, I took one last furtive look at my bed and felt anxious to be there later, as I went downstairs to the dining room.

Dinner with the family went along all right. Since I had been with them at Lake Geneva, I felt at least familiar if not "at home." Mr. Burgess was again quite formal and Ellie and her brother and sister had a lot to say to each other. It was Ellie's mother who helped me most with giving me some attention as we progressed through the meal.

The party was another matter. Without Ellie's mother, there really wasn't anyone who made me feel very much included. As hostess, Ellie needed to put her attention on her guests for the evening. I could understand that. I forced myself to enter in as much as I could, but I found myself emotionally apart and so I did a lot of observing. All of the others had been classmates of Ellie's in York High School and had gone to various colleges and universities in which some of them still studied. A number were at Northwestern University or at the University of Illinois.

At one point, Ellie came over to me with a close friend of hers she wanted me to meet. "Karl, I want you to meet Patricia Grantley. We've been best friends since grade school. . . and Pat, this is my friend from Hyde Park, Karl Swensen."

"Hello," I said.

"Hello," she said, and then looked back at some others who had come up to Ellie.

I overheard the conversation which developed among the others with Ellie and Patricia. I gathered that Patricia had recently become engaged and was to be married sometime in the spring.

It was midnight before the last guest departed. I could see how tired out Ellie was and so we agreed to meet at breakfast. I felt a pleasant relief as I closed my door behind me and made ready for bed. I consciously blocked out thoughts of the evening and put my mind to my life in Hyde Park and what l needed to do when I returned.

Ellie was at the breakfast table when I came downstairs the next morning. "Were you, pleased with the party last night, Ellie?"

"Yes. . . How about you?"

"It was good to meet your friends." I felt a certain hesitation in Ellie's consideration of the evening. I hastened to change the subject.

"Tonight is New Year's Eve. What are your plans? As you know, I'll be going back to Hyde Park today on the morning train."

"Mother and Dad have a family gathering for all of us tonight. What'll you do?"

I was evasive. "Don't know yet. . . probably not much. . . When will you be returning to school?"

"The day afer tomorrow. I've got some course work to do."

"So do I."

"When's your train, Karl?"

"In forty-five minutes, so I guess I better be getting to the station. I can just walk."

"You sure? We can find somebody to take you."

"No, I'm fine." By that time I had finished my breakfast and announced, "I'll go up and get my stuff."

When I returned downstairs with my suitcase, both Ellie and her mother were there to bid me good-bye.

"Thanks so much for a really nice time. It was so good of you to include me."

"We were glad to, Karl," her mother replied.

"Yes, Karl. Thanks for coming. I'll let you know when I get back. Maybe we can get together before everything starts up."

"Sure. . . and Happy New Year, Ellie."

We hugged and I made for the door and I began my walk of a few blocks to the Northwestern depot. Even in winter with the leaves gone, the overarching elm branches made for an impressive walk northward on Prospect. Behind me the archway extended down toward the Burgess house. *I wonder what it would have been like to have grown up here—to call this home—as in Ellie's case. And her friends whom I had seen at her party.* As I thought about this I was struck by an underlying difference between Ellie and the others. *Maybe it's because I know her so much better. But still.*

I looked at my wrist watch, and hurried to the station as I heard the train approaching. I boarded and was soon on my way to more familiar surroundings.

CHAPTER XII

I took out my key, opened my apartment door and entered. I immediately felt at ease. I closed the door behind me and put the mail I had picked up on a table next to the door. Now I felt that I was where I belonged. *It's not that the family didn't go out of its way to welcome me. None of Ellie's friends snubbed me. . .except perhaps Patricia, but then the crowd which gathered wanted to talk to her about her engagement. No—my feelings of not belonging originated in my own observations of how different Ellie's life and social context were from mine. It's not Ellie's fault, nor mine. . it's just the way it is.* With that, I put the matter out of my mind. . . at least for the time being. . .and thought of the mail which had come while I was away. There was an envelope from the Bozeman realtor, which I hastened to open.

At first reading I gathered that he was giving me the official appraisal of what my property was worth and also an estimate from a general contractor regarding complete refurbishing of the house. He then outlined a couple of options for me to consider. The first would be to sell the bulk of the farm property with the exception of the portion on which the house stood, thus providing funds adequate to refurbish the house and giving me a balance as well. The second option would be to lease the farm property, and borrow against the land value to refurbish the house. The third option was to sell the entire property. It appeared that no matter which option I would choose, I would be ahead in the long run. Of course, he concluded, I should consider the tax advantages in each case, before making my decision. He included the set of snapshots he had taken. I settled into my chair and had a long look, imagining myself as a little boy living there.

At this point, the more I thought about it the more inclined I was to hang on to the house. For no particular reason, but a sort of emotional loyalty. I found myself reclaiming my own roots which had been unknown to me until these past few weeks.

That evening I went over to Hutchison for a New Year's eve supper and then returned to my apartment without any further plans to celebrate. I would spend the evening reading. I wondered what sort of party Ellie and her family would be having. But, frankly, I was glad not to be included.

About ten o'clock, the phone rang and it was Ellie. "Hello, Karl. How are you tonight? Any plans for New Years Eve?"

"Hi, Elizabeth. I'm just here in the apartment reading. Your family party is not on yet?"

"In a couple of hours. Right before midnight."

"When do you plan to return to Hyde Park?" I felt an awkwardness between us.

"On the day after New Year's—on the 2nd. . . We could go out for supper—OK?"

"That would be good. Why don't you phone me when you get in and we'll arrange to go to supper."

"Good. . . So, until then, Happy New Year"

"Happy New Year." We hung up. I tried to go back to my reading, but I kept pondering what it was that seemed to have happened between us.

January 1, 1932

Apparently Ellie felt some of same misgiving about a change in our relationship, for in the middle of the afternoon on New Years day, she phoned me again. "Karl, what's wrong? You seemed so stiff, or maybe sad, when we talked last night. I felt so badly when we hung up."

"I know, Elizabeth. I've been pondering the same ever since. It's not you, Ellie. It's me. There were some life changing discoveries for me while I was in Montana which have left me sort of at loose ends about my life. So let's talk about all this tomorrow when you are here. Okay?"

"Maybe it's both of us. . . let's figure this out. . . I don't want to lose you."

"I don't either. . . thanks for calling me back. . . that helps me."
With that we hung up. In a little better shape, it seemed to me. *I wonder
what the new year will hold?* The next afternoon we met at a café near
the university. After preliminaries, I thrust forth. "I've been trying to
understand what happened to me . . . ."

"Tell me about it, Karl."

I hesitated as I tried to put in words what I'd been feeling. "It's an
economic, and social thing. I have come to get a better understanding of
who I am. And being with your friends, I couldn't get over the contrast
between your growing up circumstances and mine."

"I don't quite understand, Karl. As I envisioned your home and life
in Billings, it didn't seem so different from mine."

"I know, but I discovered who my birth-parents had been, and
that has shaken me up. . . I need to find out more about my roots. . . I
came from a tiny, out of the way farm in Gallatin County, Montana,
nothing at all like Billings, which is one of the big towns in the state. A
hundred and eighty degrees different from Elmhurst, where you're from.
My father had been a small time farmer. . . yours a lawyer in Chicago."

"I don't know why that should make a difference."

"I don't know either. . . but it just does. . . and then to see the house
I lived in, dilapidated and about ready for the dump. . . at least they
owned it. My stepfather had assumed that they had been renters. That's
what the meeting with the lawyer was about. . . to tell me that now I
will own it in a few years. . . Such as it is."

"You will?" Ellie exclaimed.

"Yeah, I will inherit the farm!" When I turn twenty-one I become
eligible to inherit it. The bank could not find me, but finally located
me."

"I can see why you have been in turmoil over everything you have
recently heard about your roots, Karl. . . ."

I cut in. "And I need some time to sort it out, Ellie. Be patient with
me. . . and now I need to get back and do some class prep."

"So do I. And, Karl, I'll be patient. Like I said, I don't want to
lose you." And in an attempt to part on a happier note, she added.
"Especially now that you are to be 'Lord of the Manor'!"

"Yeah, you wouldn't say that if you saw the place!"

We were silent and pensive as we left the café and walked the short distance to Ellie's apartment building. When we parted at her door I asked. "Give me some space, Ellie. I need time to re-examine my life."

"I think I need to do the same. My friend Patricia, will be planning her wedding and I'll be involved since she has asked me to be her maid of honor. But, stay in touch, Karl."

"I will."

"And, by the way, I'll be house-sitting in Uncle Roland's apartment for the next couple of weeks, like we talked about."

"Will that work for you. . .getting your course work and all?"

"Yes, there are good bus connections for me. I'll be Okay." She then gave me the phone number at the apartment.

"Thanks, we need to stay in touch, Ellie,"

"I know. Good bye for now."

CHAPTER XIII

In a few days a letter arrived in the mail from Security Bank in Bozeman telling me of a discovery of a paper which I should have, which had been written by my birth mother just before her death. It was an item which greatly interested me. It was a handwritten account of the story of my grandparents coming to Reese Creek. The note attached to this document read as follows: *Security Bank discovered this in the vault containing the papers regarding your property on Reese Creek. Apparently your mother had written this shortly before she passed away and most likely she meant it for you.*

I took this yellowed paper with barely legible hand writing in pencil. I held it in my hands as if it were holy writ. This had been written by my own mother! She wrote this for me. It was among the last things she did in her life cut short by influenza. I found an easy chair in which to read this with no distractions. I began to read. . . I imagined I was hearing a soft, loving woman's voice. . . .the voice of my mother!

SAMUEL R. AND MARGARET (BELL) ERICKSON
 After the defeat of the South, Samuel Erickson was mustered out of the army of the Confederacy. With other dislocated soldiers from Georgia he made his way to the recently discovered gold fields in Meagher County, Montana. He settled in Diamond City, which eventually was the temporary residence of 10,000 people in what was termed Confederate Gulch on the west side of the Big Belt Mountains. There he worked a claim for a while but did not strike it rich. By 1870 he moved on and worked on a number of farms in the valley south and west of Diamond

City. Samuel Erickson heard about a verdant valley further to the west where farms were said to be flourishing. He made his way westward through the Sixteen Mile Creek pass over the Bridger Mountains and southwestward into the Gallatin Valley. Sometime around 1880, he filed on a homestead on Reese Creek not far from the homestead on which John Reese had settled in 1864. He proved up, by building a log cabin and clearing land and planting a crop. That old cabin remains on our farm.

In 1884, John A. Chater, who had recently come from England established what came to be known as an "English Nobility Colony" comprising a number of log cabins he had built near the spot where later the town of Three Forks would be founded. One of the families in this cluster sent their daughter, Margaret Bell, to "The Gallatin Valley Female Seminary" located in nearby Hamilton, near what is now known as Manhattan. Under the close supervision of its principal, Mary Crittenden, her girls were permitted some social contact with approved local young men from Presbyterian churches in the area. Among these, was Samuel Erickson, a member of the Hamilton church. His homestead was a few miles to the east at Reese Creek.

In time, Samuel Erickson and Margaret Bell fell in love and eventually married. Eighteen years later, when I left my home in Minneapolis to come west to teach school in Reese Creek, I stayed in their home. That was where I met their son, Jon whom I eventually married. A year later in 1914 you were born to us. We named you Karl when you were baptized in the Presbyterian Church in Spring Hill. We three now live on the Erickson place in a house Jon and I had built for us on the original homestead. In 1917 we began raising sweet peas for a new cannery built in Bozeman to sell canned peas to feed our troops in the war in Europe. This has given us good income. But we are fearful now when we see how the Asian Flu, has affected some of our neighboring families.

----Anna Erickson, July 1918

When I came to the end and read my own mother's name, I sat in the silence of my apartment and let the "sound" of her voice linger for a few moments. I was overwhelmed as I pondered the image of my father and mother in their home holding me in their arms only days before we would no longer be together. And yet in this moment I felt for the first time in my life that I belonged, that I was truly connected. I now knew who I was—Karl Erickson of Reese Creek, Montana! Samuel and Margaret were my grandparents, the original homesteaders of the farm on which I had been born and where I lived for the first few years of my life. I felt linked to the past and to the land as I had never before felt. And the house I had seen, now in disrepair, had been my home as a child. The log cabin on the place had been my grandfather's.

I decided that I would need some time to live with this new information before drawing any conclusions as to what it would mean to me. I would not want to take any steps regarding the house and farm, now that it possessed some emotional hold upon me. Before reading my mother's account, the house and farm had little meaning other than financial. Now, suddenly it would be my place! The soil which had nourished my roots. Ellie's words "Lord of the Manor" now had some significance to me. It would be a while before I could work out the implications of my future ownership of my father and mother's house and home. Meanwhile I looked forward eagerly and somewhat impatiently to seeing my farm again.

Meanwhile, while "house sitting" for Uncle Roland, Elizabeth had been doing some soul-searching, as she would later share with me. She had not enjoyed being with her old high school friends as much as she had anticipated. She couldn't relate to their goals in life, which seemed so divergent from hers. It seemed that money and social position were of utmost significance to most of them. She, herself, felt confused as to her hopes for the future.

And then there was Patricia's wedding planning. It would be a big wedding with a most fashionable dinner and reception afterwards. It was scheduled for Saturday, June 11th, 1932. Patricia's mother had reserved First Congregational Church of Elmhurst for the ceremony. The Oak Park Arms Hotel in Oak Park would be the location for the dinner and reception. Elizabeth told me that even though the Grantleys were not Congregational they chose First Congregational because it was more fashionable than the little church they were loosely connected to.

Also they chose the Arms in Oak Park because it was the "place to go" for their social set. At the time Ellie didn't seem to think much about Grantley's choices. She told me that after the wedding she had really been "turned off" by all the display of wealth the wedding and reception would produce.

Three days before Roland was scheduled to return to Chicago, Elizabeth received a shocking phone call from her mother. "I hate to have to tell this. . . ."

"What is it, Mother?"

"Your Uncle Roland has died, while on his buying trip in South America."

"Oh, Mother. What happened?"

"We don't know all the details, but apparently he contracted some kind of serious disease, and it took his life."

"That's awful. . . Does that mean I need to stay longer here in his apartment?"

"No, dear. His lawyers will contact you this afternoon. All of Roland's affairs are in their hands and they will bring in someone to care for his apartment."

"His?"

"Yes. He owns it. It's not a rental."

"I didn't know that."

"Ellie, I have some more calls to make about my brother's affairs. But I will talk later with you about all this."

"I'm so sorry, Mother."

"I know, child."

A few days later Elizabeth received a phone call from a professional home care company informing her that they would take over the care of the apartment until such time as its ownership would transfer from Roland Whitaker's estate, and that she was now free to move back to her own apartment in Hyde Park. While this call relieved Elizabeth of her responsibility she felt a sadness to be leaving Roland's home. Since his death, this wonderful lake shore apartment was all that remained of her uncle for her. He had always been a very special person in her life. Ever since her childhood she had enjoyed sitting with her uncle looking out over the waters of Lake Michigan. She had loved to hear him tell of his travels to other parts of the world. And sometimes he would tell her of some of the "God thoughts" his view of the waters instilled in him.

A week or so after she returned to Hyde Park, she received a letter from the law firm which had charge of Roland's estate. In this letter she was asked to come to the law office to hear a reading of Roland Whitaker's last will and testament. Elizabeth's mother also received such a letter and so they would both go to the law office in the Loop together.

When the day arrived, Ellie and her mother went up the elevator to the eleventh floor occupied by Roland's lawyers. They were ushered into a mahogany-paneled conference room and were shown to seats around a large oval table. They were joined by representatives of humanitarian organizations in which Roland had had an interest. The climax of the meeting was the reading of the will. Mrs. Burgess was to receive a sizeable bequest. But the words which would long be ingrained in Elizabeth's memory were: "And to my beloved niece, Elizabeth Burgess, I bequeath my journal, *Voyage of the Spirit,* and my apartment on Lake Shore Drive, with an amount invested sufficient to care for its upkeep in the years to come." Ellie left the meeting that day overwhelmed.

Before leaving the reception area of the law offices Elizabeth and her mother sat down to discuss next steps. Her mother had been notified that Roland had been buried at sea and that sometime later the family would have a memorial service in Elmhurst. Elizabeth's father would help with the legal detail of the transfer of property to Elizabeth, but that would take a certain amount of time. Meanwhile Elizabeth would be heavily involved in completing her degree and obtaining a teaching position. Mother and daughter then left the building and went their separate ways.

When Elizabeth got back to her apartment, the first thing she did was to phone me to tell me of her inheritance. I was stunned. It made me wonder whether this development would further pull us apart. Quite a contrast between her lake shore apartment and my decrepit farm buildings. But then, the journal. What was that? In a strange way *Voyage of the Spirit* would be every bit as important as the apartment. . . or the farm, for that matter.

CHAPTER XIV

Winter and Spring 1932

When the transfer of the lake shore apartment to Elizabeth was official, she moved into the apartment, thus eliminating the expense of having a Hyde Park apartment as well.

During the remaining weeks of the academic year, both Elizabeth and I had heavy work loads and did not see very much of each other. Each of us was completing our requirements for master's degrees. Mine was in history, with which I hoped to secure a teaching position somewhere on the college level. Elizabeth had qualified herself for secondary teaching and her master's degree would enhance her preparedness to teach English and history.

If we were honest, we would have to admit that we had drifted apart somewhat since Christmas. But we kept up with various events and concerns in our lives. I shared with her what I had been doing in regard to my Montana property. As our work at the University of Chicago drew close to the end, each of us was involved in seeking a teaching position for the following year.

The deepening effects of the Great Depression had hit Chicago in ways which would affect our lives. Unemployment in manufacturing had reached 50%. Chicago public school teachers were owed as much as eight months back pay. Almost half of the black workers in the city were unemployed. It was not a good time to be looking for a teaching position.

My search for a position was focused upon Montana. As it turned out, I applied for an opening in the history department of Eastern

Montana College in Billings from which I had my bachelor's degree. At that time it was mainly a preparatory school for teachers. Immediately after graduation I would need to go to Billings for an interview.

Elizabeth heard of an English teaching position at Lincoln Park High School on the near north side of Chicago, not far from her new address on Lake Shore Drive. One of her professors at the U.of C. had called her to alert her to an opening at Lincoln Park due to a sudden death of an English teacher. Elizabeth made an appointment and went up to see about the position and if possible to apply for it. The principal informed her. "We cannot pay the salary in full. In fact we are behind in paying all our teachers, but if you can live with that we might be able to take you on."

"Yes, I think I can. It would mean a lot to me just to be hired at this point."

The principal examined Elizabeth's résumé and her application. "Your material looks good. Give me until Monday, and I will let you know."

"Thank you, sir."

It seemed like a very long weekend, but on Monday the call came through offering her the job.

As these plans became finalized, we both had to face the fact that we might be a long distance from each other. This would force us to determine what our relationship—if any—would be. In a curious way, Patricia's wedding would play a significant part in that determination.

Mr. Swensen returns to the present to resume
his teaching at Elmhurst College.

Elmhurst 1948

As the Chicago Northwestern commuter train pulled into the depot, Mr. Swensen folded up his Tribune, rose from his seat and took hold of his suitcase to prepare to step off the passenger car and begin his short walk to the campus and to his room on the third floor of Old Main. It was Sunday evening, and in the morning he would once again resume his weekly schedule of classes.

After his first class, he returned to his room, took away the *Return on Monday* sign, kept his door open for visitors and went to his cluttered desk. Soon after he was settled, Maynard came through the open doorway. "Hello, Mr. Otterberg.

"Hello, Mr. Swensen. I have another question about our assignment, which I hope you can clear up for me."

"Certainly. What is it?"

With that, Maynard explained his question and Mr. Swensen reinterpreted the matter to Maynard's satisfaction.

"Thank you very much, sir." He hesitated as he made for the door.

"What is it, Maynard. Do you have further questions?"

"I have been wondering about your doctoral hood hanging there on your gown. What institution are those colors for?"

"Oh, I received my Ph.D. from the University of Chicago a few year's ago."

"Oh, I didn't know. We should be calling you Dr. Swensen, then."

"No, I'd rather you used the 'Mr.' As it was after my master's degree which was also from the University of Chicago. However, my B.A. was from Eastern Montana College.

Neither had anything else to say so Maynard got up to leave. "Well, thank you, sir."

When Maynard returned to his dorm room, Dale was at his desk studying. "Did you find him?"

"Yes, and he set me straight." He then told Dale about the doctoral hood from the University of Chicago, but his bachelor's was from Montana.

"That explains why he has his field study set for Montana."

"And another thing I noticed."

"What was that?"

"He wears a small gold ring with a little diamond embedded in it. On his ring finger like he's married."

"But, he's a bachelor. . . or so we thought. . . ."

After Maynard left the office, Karl Swensen leaned back in his desk chair, clasped his hands behind his head, and closed his eyes . *Yes, University of Chicago. . . commencement. . .master's degree hood. . . Afterwards with Elizabeth. . . she with her hood, was surrounded by her parents and family. . . later that evening when her family left to return to Elmhurst, she and I went out to eat a late snack. . . We talked about*

Roland's unbelievable gifts to her as directed in his will. Not only the apartment, but the journal. . . She talked about Patricia's wedding. . .she wasn't looking forward to it. . . Patricia's parents had turned it into a glamorous social event to enhance their own standing among their friends and business connections. Elizabeth couldn't wait to begin her teaching job at Lincoln Park.

The following Saturday Karl would be in his lake shore apartment, once again continuing his story.

CHAPTER XV

Mr. Swensen writes more of the story of his earlier days

Elmhurst,. June, 1932

The week after Elizabeth and I each received our master's degrees at the University of Chicago commencement exercise, we went our separate ways – temporarily. While I made my trip to Billings to interview at Eastern Montana College, Elizabeth moved back to her parents' home in Elmhurst temporarily after signing a contract for the following year at Lincoln Park High. She then became heavily involved in Patricia's wedding a few days later.

The ceremony concluded at four o'clock on Saturday, June 11 as Elizabeth, as maid of honor, lifted the bride's veil after the couple was pronounced husband and wife and the newly wedded couple kissed. The organ burst forth with the recessional as Elizabeth stooped to adjust the long train on Patricia's gown before the couple began their triumphal walk down the aisle to the double doors of the sanctuary, with the full congregation standing to honor their marriage. The ushers flung open the doors, and the bride and groom were helped into the rear seat of the waiting white Packard open limousine with a uniformed chauffeur. The magnificent machine drove away from the church and headed south to St. Charles Road with a parade of vehicles following with their horns blowing.

Eight miles and a half an hour later, the wedding coach pulled up to the canopied entrance of the Oak Park Arms Hotel on Oak Park Avenue. A uniformed doorman helped the couple into the lobby, where the catering manager led them into the lounge where a reception line was forming, Soon the lobby was filling up with guests waiting to greet the wedding party. Elizabeth had to be greeted by all who came by her in the line. She quickly became weary of the required ritual. She observed that most of the people she greeted were Patricia's parents' friends and business associates of her father. The grand piano in the lobby outside the French window facing the Main Dining Room could be heard playing during the receiving line and later during the dinner following.

The group mingled in the lounge until the doors to the Main Dining Room were opened and everyone moved into the elegant room and took their places ready to be served a complete five course prime rib dinner. After the dinner, the room was cleared and a band took its place to begin playing for the dance, which would last until midnight when the catering manager blinked the lights in the ballroom to signal the closing of the evening's celebration. All the while a bar set up by the family would serve drinks continually, much to the consternation of those who would need to drive home and those who would find Sunday morning a painful blur.

By the end of the evening the bride and groom had left. Those who remained were quite impressed with the whole affair which Patricia's parents had ostentatiously sponsored for their friends and associates. An impression which Elizabeth did not share as she and her parents left the hotel around ten o'clock to return to Elmhurst.

While Elizabeth was enduring Patricia's wedding, I was in Billings to interview at Eastern Montana College. I no longer had a residence in Billings, since my adoptive parents had retired and moved to Iowa to care for "Mother's" widowed mother. Their move, together with my birth mother's letter to me before her death, put a pall over Billings for me as I checked into the Lincoln Hotel on 1st Avenue North. It wasn't my town anymore, if it ever had been, and as I prepared to meet the committee at Eastern, I found myself strangely uninterested in going to Billings to teach. I will never know, but this shift in mood may have affected the outcome of the interview.When the interview was over, the chairman indicated that I would receive a letter in a few days with the results of the committee's decision.

The next day, l was on the train speeding back to Chicago, with mixed emotions about the entire experience. Returning to my Hyde Park apartment without any further university responsibilities, I was at loose ends, not knowing what was next in my life, much less where I would be living. I felt as though I needed to share my thoughts with Elizabeth.

The next morning I phoned Elizabeth. "Hello Ellie. . . I got back last night. . . no, I have not yet gotten word from the interview committee. . . So, how was the wedding?"

"Karl, it was a big gaudy show in my opinion, but everyone seemed to have a marvelous time. It's too much to try and tell you on the phone. Frankly, I was turned off by it."

"And did you get a job at Lincoln Park?"

"Yes, I did, and I am thrilled."

"Good for you. I'd like to see you, but I need to wait for a letter from the Billings committee. . .in a day or two, I think. . . Yes, as soon as I hear I'll phone you." I hung up. Nothing to do but wait. And while I waited I went back and forth in my thinking. On the one hand I needed the job, but on the other hand I had no interest in living in Billings again. In the back of my mind was my heart. I wanted to be closer to Ellie.

CHAPTER XVI

The letter finally arrived. After routine preliminaries, it informed me that there were no full time positions open to me, but that I could possibly be given a part time visiting instructor course or two as needed in the history department. I wrote a "thanks, but no thanks" reply. Despite the rejection, I felt a hidden relief. I would be able to remain in the Chicago area. . . near Ellie.

I phoned Ellie at her home in Elmhurst. "Hello, Ellie. I have gotten word from Billings. . . No, they do not have a position for me, only a few courses possibly on a visiting instructor basis. . . No, I do not want that. I need a full position. . . I don't know. I'd like to see you and we can talk about what other options I may have."

"Karl, I want to see you too. I fact I was hoping I might show you my new apartment."

"I'd like that."

"How about first thing tomorrow? I am coming in to my apartment in the morning. We can meet at the Northwestern station when my train comes in at 8:30 and could grab a bus and go up to the apartment."

"Good. I'll pick you up at the station at 8:30."

The next morning, Saturday, we stepped off the bus after a short ride, walked a few bocks to Lake Shore Drive and entered the glass doors of a high rise apartment building facing the lake. The uniformed doorman greeted Ellie, "Hello, Miss Burgess."

"Hello, Arthur. This is my friend, Karl Swensen."

An elevator took us to the sixteenth floor. Elizabeth took out her key as we approached No. 1619. We walked into a spacious living room. Ellie stepped to the window opposite the entry door and pulled open the drapes to expose a floor to ceiling window overlooking the lapping waves of Lake Michigan below and beyond their building.

I was taken aback. "What a magnificent view!"

"Isn't it though! Roland loved it and I do too, ever since I first sat here as a little girl."

"And I can see why."

Ellie and I took the two easy chairs poised to look out onto the lake. As with Roland before them, there was something magical about concentrating on the lake beneath them—soothing and enlivening at the same time.

After a few minutes of silence Ellie asked. "Tell me about your letter from the college in Billings."

"Not much to tell. They don't have a position for me. I can't manage on a few courses here and there, which they said might be possible."

"That's too bad. What will you do now?"

"I'm not sure. The curious thing about it is that I am glad I won't be going to Montana. I really want to stay in this area. . . find something here."

"Why not Montana?"

"Well, if you really want to know. . . I missed being near you, Ellie."

"That's sweet, Karl. . . It's kind of strange. Where we settle is linked to whom we want to be near. I always thought I'd want to teach at York High in Elmhurst, but then after Patricia's wedding, I was repulsed by all the forced glamour and artificiality, to say nothing of seeing a lot of my old acquaintances weaving around with too much drink. I couldn't wait to get back to Hyde Park, and to this city on the lake. Now just to sit here in the quiet of this room and to peer out onto the waters is such a relief. . . and to think that this is mine!"

"Yes, and you have a teaching position not far from here. What could be better!"

"To have you find job somewhere in this region."

"Yeah. But where?"

Elizabeth appeared to be deep in thought. I took my eyes off the lake and turned to Ellie. "What are you thinking?"

"I was just wondering about Elmhurst College. . . Wouldn't it be great if you got a position there?"

"Never thought of that. I really don't know anything about the college. . . Might be worth a try. . . Say, by the way, what did you find in that journal your uncle left you."

"I haven't read much of it, but it contains his thoughts over the years as he has looked out over the sea, or in the case of his apartment—over the lapping waves of the lake. In it he has recorded many of his 'God thoughts.' Now when I sit in his lake shore window, I can still hear him tell me his God thoughts. It starts a long way back when he first entered the Merchant Marines. He did a sketch on the first page of an ancient sailing ship called *The Spirit*. And then on the first page he quoted this old Hymn:

> *Jesus, Saviour, pilot me*
> *Over Life's Tempestuous sea;*
> *Unknown waves before me roll,*
> *Hiding rock and treacherous shoal:*
> *Chart and compass come from Thee:*
> *Jesus Saviour, pilot me.*

John E. Gould, 1871

CHAPTER XVII

October of 1932

I was happily settled into a new routine of teaching three history courses at Elmhurst College after having had a very constructive interview with President Timothy Lehmann. I appeared in his office just at the time he was looking for a history professor. "Yes, we are looking for an addition to our faculty in history."

"Thank you, I am very interested, sir."

"However, there is a proviso. We are in the process of applying for accreditation and for that we need to add Ph.D.'s to our faculty. Is there a chance that you might be planning on going for a doctorate?"

"Eventually."

"Could you begin that process at this point?"

"I certainly will consider that, if it is a requirement for this position?"

"Good, as soon as you make a commitment to a Ph.D. program, let me know and we can proceed with your application."

"Thank you, Dr. Lehmann. I will be glad to do that."

I returned to the University of Chicago and made the necessary arrangements to enter a Ph.D. track. I was accepted at Elmhurst and a schedule of courses was worked out so that I could work on my doctorate in as rapid a time as possible. I was given a room on an upper floor of the Old Main, and meals in the Commons as well in lieu of an adequate salary, which due to the depression, would not be available.

Now, both Ellie and I were well established in the beginning weeks of our careers, and enjoying contact with each other as often as possible, sometimes in her apartment on the lake, and occasionally in Elmhurst when she came out to see her parents. For a while after Patricia's extravagant wedding, Ellie had felt estranged from her family roots, perceiving that her father wanted to make something of a show of his wealth and position, something like the Grantleys.

However, the ripple effect of the stock market crash of '29 had finally been felt in her father's firm. His own income had been restricted accordingly, which was having a humbling effect upon him. This financial downfall in a curious way brought Ellie back to me. Furthermore, I found that Ellie's parents had come to accept me more fully, and as the months progressed we often spent Sundays together attending church and going to her parents' house for Sunday dinner together. As Ellie and I spent more and more of our time together we grew to be the best of friends. We especially enjoyed spending vacations in the summers with her family at the cabin.

On my low depression salary, I was constantly pinching pennies, while hoping to have enough in the bank to ask Ellie to marry me. I projected that it could take a while before I had enough. As the months passed my bank account improved. Meanwhile, Ellie's birthday on October 23, 1933 fell on a Saturday, which gave us opportunity to celebrate throughout the day and evening. Her parents planned to have us in their home on Sunday to celebrate. On that Friday afternoon, I met her at the Elmhurst train station. She was delighted to come home for the birthday weekend. Later that evening would be our special time together.

We went to The Spinning Wheel on Ogden Avenue in Hinsdale for dinner. Ellie's brother had loaned me his car which he was not using at school. The decor and architecture of the restaurant was that of a Southern plantation mansion dining room. The waitresses wore full length flowered dresses while period kerosene lamps burned on each table, casting a warm glow throughout the room. Elizabeth had been to the Spinning Wheel with her parents. She took great delight in introducing it to me as we turned off the road and drove deep into a lane leading to a tree lined entrance surrounded by lawn and gardens. After parking we walked a short distance to the front porch of the restaurant, mounted the steps and crossed over to the entry door where we were met by a hostess who showed us to a table for two.

The meal was the most delicious I had ever had, but more than that, the entire occasion for both of us was a very special turning point in our relationship. After dessert over coffee, I looked into Ellie's eyes with the sparkling reflection of the oil lamp enlivening her in a way I had never seen. I reached out and took her hand while Ellie also seemed to be overwhelmed. Without saying a word we nodded in a way that mystically assured each of us that we wanted to marry. She looked across the table into my eyes and whispered, "How soon?"

"As soon as my bank account grows a bit."

We drove back to her home almost as if in a trance. At her door we kissed more deeply than we had ever done before. Before we parted I said. "May I meet you tomorrow after lunch? There is an errand on which I'd like for you to come with me."

"Of course. Sounds mysterious."

"It is!"

The next day after lunch I picked Ellie up at her house. "Happy birthday, sweetheart."

"Oh, Karl! Thank you."

We drove to a jewelry store on York Street. "This is where I want to buy your birthday present."

"Oh?"

"Yes, a ring to signify our intention to marry!"

"You sure?"

"Of course. Will you accept it?"

"Of course!"

We selected a plain gold band with a small diamond embedded in a slightly wide spot at the center of the band. It fitted her nicely. When it was removed and wrapped I took the precious package. "This is mine! Until I present it to you at your party his evening." With that we left to take Ellie home for the afternoon. "Will your father be at home?"

"No, he has to be at the office until four."

"Do you have his office phone number?"

"Yes." Knowingly, she wrote it on a slip of paper to give to me before she went into her house. We kissed and I returned to my office on campus, where I phoned Mr. Burgess. "May I meet you at the station here in Elmhurst. I'd like to speak with you and I can give you a ride home."

"Yes, Karl. It will be about 4:30."

I arrived at the station ten minutes early and paced back and forth on the platform until the commuter train arrived and Mr. Burgess stepped off.

"Hello, Mr. Burgess. I have a car in front of the depot."

"Hello, Karl. Good of you to meet me."

When we both were in the car, I did not start up the engine until I had a chance to speak to Ellie's father. "I know this is rather sudden, but I want to ask you before Elilzabeth's birthday party this evening."

"What's that?"

"I want to ask your approval of my marrying your daughter."

"What does she say, Karl?"

"She would like that very much."

"Do you love her in a way that, to the best of your knowledge, will last a lifetime?"

"Yes, sir, Mr. Burgess."

"Well, then, you may call me *Dad* instead of Mr. Burgess." he replied joyfully. "Elizabeth's mother and I will be very happy for you two." We drove to the Burgess residence, both with a smile.

"I have appreciated your asking me for Ellie's hand."

"Thank you. . . Dad."

CHAPTER XVIII

Elmhurst 1932

It was a simple birthday dinner with Ellie and her parents. Ellie had requested her favorite home cooked meal of meat loaf and scalloped potatoes. Chocolate cake and ice cream of course with presents afterwards. The climax was my gift of the engagement ring to Elizabeth and all that such a gift signified.

Ellie squealed with delight as I placed her simple gold band with an embedded diamond on her finger. We spontaneously kissed. Her mother and father looked on happily. Her parents spoke of the time when they had become engaged. I looked at the ring on her mother's finger and said. "And that is the very ring all these year's later."

She looked embarrassed when she replied. "No. Those were simpler times. When my husband became well established he bought me this ring which is much larger than the original. More like the rings our friends were wearing. . . that was about the same time we built this house, after having lived in a small bungalow in Forest Park."

Mr. Burgess had a sadly wistful look when he entered the conversation. "Yes, those were simpler times. . . good times, though. When we didn't have much. . .and it didn't matter so much that others were better off. Now, look at us. Since the crash of '29 none of us is well off anymore. What does it matter how big a ring you wear or what sort of house we live in. Just so we can keep your head above water."

The room was quiet until Elizabeth spoke. "I have been reading in Uncle Roland's journal and something I read last night sort of fits."

"What did he write?" her mother asked somewhat plaintively.

Elizabeth went up to her room and brought down the journal, and began reading.

When I look out upon the water I am struck by its buoyancy. It holds the ships of the sea in its strong arms. The buoyant sea allows those who sail upon its dangerous waves to pass from shore to shore no matter how far apart these may be. Bringing Columbus to our shores from Spain long ago, and the Pacific Islanders in their long boats to the islands of New Zealand a thousand years ago.

I see in this remarkable buoyancy of the waters the redeeming buoyancy of God who lovingly carries us "over life's tempestuous sea." Indeed I believe the buoyancy of the sea will carry me home someday"

Mr. Burgess appeared to be deep in thought and then shared some of his musings. "You know, that word *buoyancy* makes sense to me. In these rough times since the crash, so many of my friends feel as though they are at sea and feel like they are going to sink. I even wonder if that is what went through the minds of those who committed suicide after losing everything. Thank God I found God's buoyancy through coming to a deeper experience in church these past few years."

Elizabeth turned to her dad and said, "Oh, Daddy, what you have told us is a wonderful birthday gift for me. I am so glad that you have found your way though these tough times."

"We both have, dear," her mother added.

In later life I would look back on the weeks following Ellie's birthday party and our engagement as some of the happiest in my life.

We were able to spend most weekends together, some in Elmhurst, but more often I went in to Chicago for the day on Saturday or Sunday. On many a Sunday I arrived early enough for us to go to church together. Ellie had found the Lincoln Park Presbyterian Church on Fullerton to be a cordial group of people and the preacher most provocative. After some weeks she joined the church. She offered her services to the Sunday School. After church we would find a restaurant for our noon meal and then do some hiking in Lincoln Park, particularly along the lake shore when the weather was good. Some Sunday afternoons, especially in the winter, we took the bus to Grant Park where we visited the museums in that region.

But many of the best times were when we relaxed in the lake shore apartment and sat looking out "Uncle Roland's" window. During these times of quiet meditation, Elizabeth would often take Roland's journal and read an entry or two out loud for each of us to ponder. Little did I know it, but the time would come when his thoughts would become singularly precious to me, remembering our moments of reading as we sat before "Uncle Roland's" window. I had cause later to read and re-read this entry.

When I have been at sea for some period of time, I often think of sailors over the centuries who have been separated from their families for years at a time, especially in the fifteenth century age of explorations into far-off unknown waters. I have been spared some of that pain by not being married, but I see the pain of long separation in others at times. However there was Mandy in Dunedin, New Zealand. We were only together briefly but when I had to return to the ship, we pledged to see each other next time. But the next time was a year later, and she was gone. I've never met another like her. The sea is now a more lonely place for me.

Ellie and I were experiencing the best months of our lives as autumn with its blazing colors gradually turned into early winter. I spent a cozy "down-home" Thanksgiving with the Burgess family at their cabin on Lake Geneva.

Christmas was especially joyous in Elmhurst with Ellie and her family. I joined Ellie and her family in their church for a "midnight" Christmas Eve service. And then on a crisp Christmas morning, I walked from my rooms on campus to Ellie's house under the stately elms whose branches were clothed in fresh white arching over streets and lawns covered in snow. A post card-perfect setting for a most memorable celebration. That evening Ellie and I were alone in her living room by the soft lights of the Christmas tree. "It feels so good to be home, Karl! Don't you think?"

I pondered her declaration and then said. "Ellie, I don't really know. Your full and beautiful feeling of home is not something I have in my background. Having never really known my parents and their home on Reese Creek. . . and as I have said to you before, my stepparents, though I'm sure they meant well, just didn't know how to make their house a home in that full sense which you declare." After saying this, I didn't feel good about having been so critical of my past. . . .but still. And yet my being here in Elmhurst and its surroundings does, in fact, touch me emotionally in a way I have never before felt.

A week later Ellie and I were ensconced in the Burgess living room before a fire in the fireplace awaiting the midnight bells of the new year.

January 1, 1933. It would be the year of our marriage, we proclaimed to each other. But the ceremony, we found, would not be as planned.

Winter progressed in its frozen splendor until the spring sunshine began to melt the icy streets and soon we began to see crocuses popping out of the flower beds in front of the Burgess house. Each of us began to be quite involved in winding up our school year of teaching. But by the end of May we were free to engage in summer delights.

We celebrated the beginning of our summer holiday by taking a stroll in Wilder Park across the street from Elmhurst College. After walking through the greenhouse filled with blooming flowers, we sat on a bench in the outside garden. We both knew that we wanted to discuss our plans. We settled upon the first Saturday in August for our wedding. "I don't want a big showy wedding," Ellie declared, and I agreed.

"Just a maid of honor and a best man would be fine with me," I said.

"But I would like it to be in my church. . . We need to get in touch with my pastor, to make arrangements before we decide further details."

"Fine with me. . . Whom do you want for your maid of honor?"

"My friend, Julia, who teaches at Lincoln Park. How about you?"

"There is a new part-time German teacher at the college, Rudolf Bauer, whose friendship I have come to enjoy."

The following week we met with Ellie's pastor and arranged for our wedding. Each of our teacher friends agreed and told us how thrilled they were for us. Further details could be set later.

In the months before our wedding, Ellie and I planned to visit The Century of Progress World's Fair in Chicago multiple times in order to take it all in. As it turned out we would have only one long day visit.

We rode a blue and white streamlined train with open cars which drove on the side walks on rubber tires. In this way we could go from display to display and into many of the Fair buildings. The exhibits came from many countries of the world, offering products from their own country. Cuckoo clocks from Germany, cut glassware from Czechoslovakia, brightly colored clothing items from Mexico and other South American countries—on and on it went. A wide variety of food vendors offered indigenous foods from many parts of the world. We had lunch "in Mexico" and dinner served in a French café. In the evening we sat before a lagoon, at which some steel drummers performed. It was dusk, and a multitude of lights reflected upon the lagoon making the nearly black water seem silvery. Out of the blue, Ellie turned to me. "Oh, Karl, I want to see the ocean. I want to look out onto the sea as Uncle Roland did so often in his life."

"We will do that some day, dear, I promise you."

"I'll take his journal and read it as I look over the waters."

I would long remember her wish. . . and my promise.

We were both tired by the end of the day. But somehow, Ellie seemed more than tired to me. And when we boarded a bus to take us to Lincoln Park, Ellie appealed to me. "Karl, get me home as quickly as you can. I don't feel at all well. We arrived at her building and went up to her apartment. She took two aspirins. I helped her to her bed. She complained of chills and was shivering. I covered her up with as many blankets as she had. "Don't leave me, Karl." she cried.

"I'll stay right here. I can sleep on your couch and you can call me whenever you need me."

"Thank you, sweetheart,." she said as she closed her eyes.

I was worried. At 5:30 she awakened me. "Karl. I need your help."

I helped her to the bathroom. When she came out, she went back to her bed. "Are you any better?"

"A little, but I think I want to be at home with Mother. Could you call my parents?"

"Certainly." I awakened them, but when I explained the situation, Mr Burgess said. "I will come for her as soon as I possibly can. Can you have her ready in forty-five minutes?"

"Yes, we will be ready. Thank you so much."

I helped Ellie get dressed as best as I could. When the time drew near, I wrapped her in her winter coat and we waited for her father. He made it in record time and together we helped Ellie into her father's car. He drove down Michigan Avenue to Washington Boulevard. He drove at a speed which enabled him to hit most of the traffic lights on green. When I remarked about that, he said, "I learned that some years ago when I needed to get to the office as quickly as possible."

Fortunately, Ellie slept all the way. When we arrived we both helped her into the house and up to her old bedroom. He mother phoned the family doctor and he came within the hour. He asked some questions of Ellie and checked her heart and lungs with his stethoscope. He turned to he mother and said, "She needs to be in the hospital. I'll phone for an ambulance."

"What is her trouble?" Her mother asked, obviously very worried.

"I can't say at this point, her heart needs stabilizing."

Soon the ambulance arrived. She was carefully moved onto a Gurney and she was cautiously loaded her into the ambulance. As she was whisked away to the local Elmhurst hospital, I accompanied the Burgesses in their car. We waited in the emergency room. I felt very much a member of the family, more so than ever before.

CHAPTER XIX

Elmhurst–Summer, 1933

During the first week of her hospitalization, Ellie was heavily sedated. The family doctor, in consultation with a heart specialist, explained to the family that Ellie's serious illness in childhood had done some damage to her heart, which now had caused a heart condition which resembled a heart attack. When her mother had asked the doctors what to expect, they were non-committal. "We must wait and see how she does in her recovery from this event. All we can do is to give her complete bed rest."

"Do you mean at home?" her father asked.

"No, I think we should keep her here so that we can monitor her heart condition closely in the coming weeks."

"Can she have visitors?" I was anxious to know.

"Yes, if you don't stay too long and wear her out."

And so our time together would be limited as I took turns with Ellie's mother during the visiting hours in the afternoons and in the evening visiting hours with Mr. Burgess. This constraint drew Ellie and me closer and deeper. We found ourselves revealing more and more little tidbits of memories of our childhoods. One which I would remember long into the future was about a little favorite doll of hers with which she "lived" imaginary scenes and events. When I asked. "What sort of scenes do you mean?" she answered. "Oh, we would walk in the forest, or go to the ocean shore to see with the waves coming toward us-- one after another."

"Do you still have that doll?"

"Oh, yes. She is always near my pillow—even today!"

"I'd like to see her."

"I'll ask Mother to bring her next time she comes to the hospital." Then Ellie became quiet and pensive. "Oh Karl, I would so like to see the ocean shore, to watch the waves come in. I have only "seen" it with my dolly."

"Some day, after you're out of here, we'll go to the sea shore together, you and me. . .and you can take your dolly!"

Ellie smiled, closed her eyes and drifted off to sleep.

The next day when we were alone in her room she showed me her doll. "This is Elizabeth!" And handed me a slender doll dressed like a teenager with hair the color of Ellie.

"Mom also brought Uncle Roland's journal." She pointed to the book on a side table. I picked it up and paged through it, finding a page marked with a book mark. I read it aloud.

The sea is mesmerizing. It is magical. Gazing out at the endless incoming waves makes me feel timeless. Mighty waves keep coming to shore where they disappear leaving the sand wet and shiny, often depositing shells from who knows how far away.. One after another. . . after another. . . another. . . from whence do they come? From a far off shore. . . far, far, away. . .from a far off shore of another continent. . .another world. . . a world unseen. . . and yet a world made and loved by God as surely as God loves my world.. . . .

"Some day, sweetheart, I'll read you these words as you gaze at the incoming waves of the sea." Ellie smiled, reached out her hand for mine. . . and went to sleep. I vowed to keep my word, no matter what.

As the day of our wedding approached we spoke more and more with each other about our wedding, hoping so much that she would be improved enough to be released from the hospital. Fortunately the family doctor shared our hope, even though her condition seemed to have stabilized at abut the same level.

A week before the wedding, the doctor examined Ellie extensively and concluded, " I think we can let you go to the church for your wedding. . . if you let me attend?" he said with a glint in his eye.

"Of course." was Ellie's answer.

"And, let's have a wheel chair handy, just in case you need to sit down."

As the doctor left the room, he asked me to come into the hall with him. When we were alone with a knowing look, he said to me in a most kindly way. "I'm sorry, but you will need to wait until she has improved a bit more. . . know what I mean?"

"I understand, Doctor."

And so it would be. Nevertheless we were ecstatic.

We then began to make our final arrangements. It would be a private ceremony in the early afternoon with a meal in the Burgess home afterwards, before Ellie would need to be returned to her hospital room. Both Julie and Rudolf were so very happy for us.

However, two days before our wedding date, Ellie took a serious turn for the worst, prompting the Doctor to tell us. "I cannot in good faith let you leave the hospital. . . I am so sorry."

After digesting this disappointing word, I asked as I held Ellie's hand, "Could we have the marriage performed here in the room?" I could feel her hand tighten in mine.

He thought this over and said, "I think you could. . . if her condition remains stable."

"Thank you," was all I could say as tears began to form in my eyes.

"And I think you need to let her sleep now. You can see her this evening."

I leaned over and kissed Ellie before leaving.

On the morning of our wedding, the nurses brought in vases of cut flowers and helped Ellie into her wedding gown as best as they could while she still lay in bed. Rudolph Bauer, and Julia Meyers stood outside in the hall to greet me as I approached in my wedding suit, accompanied by Mr. and Mrs. Burgess. It was a solemn, yet joyful gathering as we waited for Pastor Crowley. When he came down the corridor dressed in his clerical gown I felt a surge of emotion through my body and moisture in my eyes. We quietly greeted him and then processed into Ellie's room, where Doctor Otis stood in the corner with his professional eye and kindly heart in constant attention. Two nurses stood ready to assist if needed.

I stood by her bed, accompanied by her parents, as the pastor began.

We are here in the presence of God and before these witnesses to unite Elizabeth and Karl in holy marriage. . . .

When the time came the pastor asked.

Who giveth Elizabeth to be married to Karl?

Her mother and I do. They placed her hand in mine.

The vows followed, ending in these prophetic words: *as long as we both shall live.* I replied "I will. . . and forever after."

"Thus I pronounce you husband and wife by the law of the state and the love of God. Amen."

To everyone's surprise, just before the benediction, Rudolph Bauer sang.

> *As a mother stills her child,*
> *Thou canst hush the ocean wild:*
> *Boisterous waves obey Thy will*
> *When Thou sayest to them, "Be still!"*
> *Wondrous Sovereign of the sea,*
> *Jesus, Saviour, pilot these.*

By common unspoken consent, everyone left the room for Ellie and me to quietly share our undying love with a mutual kiss. Having whispered to me earlier, the nurses brought in a cot for me to spend the night with Ellie.

I stood close to the side of her bed and held her hand. We were quiet as we sensed a closeness we had never before experienced. I felt as though her being was flowing into me as my being merged with hers. Finally I broke the silence. "Dear sweet Ellie, love of my life, what are you thinking?"

She looked to me with glowing moist eyes. After a long moment she spoke softly. "It won't be long, dear. . . I must leave you for a time. . . ."

I felt like interrupting, but something held me back. . . I allowed Ellie to continue.

"I want to tell you what I anticipate." She waited for me to indicate that I wanted her to tell me. "This is what I believe is coming:

"For me the most insightful and hope-filled look ahead is the statement by John in Revelation. When I was in Confirmation class we memorized his words:

See, the home of God is with mortals. He will dwell with them; they shall be his people, and God himself shall be with them; and be their God. And God shall wipe away all tears from their eyes; and there shall be no more death, neither sorrow, nor crying, neither shall there be any more pain: for the former things are passed away.

"Whatever has been good and beautiful this side of the grave will be, I believe, good and beautiful beyond our ability to imagine. Whatever here has been negative in any way will simply not be any longer present. All that hurt or destroyed happiness will be gone forever. Sorrow for our losses here will be replaced with infinite joy. Death will be replaced with infinite life. Thus loved ones lost will be with us in a way we cannot even begin to imagine.

"And most of all. . . you and I will be together and we will be at home with God without any separation!"

"Oh, Ellie. . . yes—yes—yes. . . ." She had drifted into sleep. . . softly smiling.

I leaned over and gave her a "good night" kiss. I tiptoed over to my cot. When in bed I whispered a prayer. *She is Yours, Oh God.* Each of us slept in peace.

The next morning a nurse came in to attend to Ellie. I got up and prepared to leave the room. After waiting in the hall for a few minutes the nurse came out. " You can go back in to her, Karl." When I again stood by Ellie's bed she smiled weakly, held out her hand for me to take, and asked pathetically, "Can I have Elizabeth?" At first I was confused. " But you are Elizabeth."

"That's my dolly's name."

I saw the doll on the window sill and brought it to her. "Here she is." Ellie took the doll and held it to her chest. She looked to me with plaintive eyes. "Karl, dear, take me to the ocean shore." Then she spread a flat place on her bed sheet, and put the doll at the edge of the flat spot and said in a child-like voice. "Elizabeth is looking out to sea. . . she is happy." I watched this child's drama unfold and then Ellie closed her eyes and fell asleep

I leaned over and kissed her cheek and whispered in her ear. "I will, Ellie."

The next day, I turned my attention to the house on Reese Creek. In the midst of the ordeal I was facing with Ellie's severe illness my twenty-first birthday had come and gone without any attention given to it. However, Mr. Sutherland, the Bozeman attorney had written me to invite me to come to Bozeman to formally receive my inheritance.

I knew that I needed to respond to my lawyer regarding the disposition of the property. I knew now that I wanted to keep the house and renovate it, in order to bring it back to what it must have been like when I had lived there as a small child. The funds I would need to accomplish this redevelopment would have to come from the sale of the farmland. It was at this point in my thinking that I felt some discouragement, due to the economic downturn which the depression had brought.

In the meantime I wrote to Mr. Sutherland explaining my personal involvement with my wife's illness and asked him to hold off any action regarding my inheritance until her recovery would permit me to come to Bozeman.

A week and a half later I was in my office when the phone rang. It was Ellie's nurse. "Karl, you need to come to the hospital. Your wife is failing fast." When I got to Ellie's room, I found she was lying on the bed unconscious still clutching her doll. The nurse greeted me with a sympathetic knowing look.

Her parents arrived soon after I had entered the room. The nurse had phoned them and their pastor as well. He came close behind the Burgess'es. Rudolf also entered the room. Apparently word had reached him at the college.

All of us gathered around the bed, and held hands as the pastor recited the twenty-third Psalm, and then offered a deeply felt prayer. After the prayer there was a silence. Then Ralph began to sing.

> When at last I near the shore,
> And the fearful breakers roar
> 'Twixt me and the peaceful rest,
> Then while leaning on thy breast,
> May I hear Thee say to me,
> "Fear not, I will pilot thee."

We stood in respectful quiet. I looked intently on the blanket covering Ellie. I could see faintly a slight movement of her breathing. And then she became motionless. Ellie's doll dropped to the floor. The pastor offered a closing prayer.

CHAPTER XX

Mr. Swensen has concluded the story of his earlier years.

Chicago 1948

A few of Mr. Swensen's tears dropped onto the paper on which he had been writing, smearing the ink from his fountain pen. He carefully closed the notebook and put down his pen. This would be his final entry. He leaned back and stared down at the gentle waves of Lake Michigan splashing onto the shore. He felt what he had often felt. An impossible wish to return to an earlier time in his life.

His eye fell on a small table at the edge of the tall lake view window. He spotted Uncle Roland's journal, Ellie's favorite doll, "Elizabeth," and a snapshot of Ellie. There was the Bible she had used Confirmation class and a tiny gold cross mounted in a polished wooden base. This was a sort of shrine at which he had sometimes prayed.

As Karl looked at the doll he prayed. . . Then he seemed to hear Ellie's words again.

"Karl, dear, take me to the ocean." Karl uttered aloud his response, "I will, Ellie." Her plaintive cry prompted Karl to take Roland's journal down and to start to page through it. He came across an early entry.

The very first time I saw an ocean was when our family lived in Portland, Oregon. We had gone by horse drawn carriage to Cannon Beach. I was totally captivated when I first stood on the sand and looked out onto the sea as the waves rolled in one after another. I was a small boy at the time but I think this experience set me on a pathway to a life at sea. I inherited a wanderlust from my grandparents who had come west on the Oregon Trail from Missouri to the Willamette Valley in what is now Oregon. And I must have decided then and there to continue their westward journey onto the sea to the far-flung corners of the earth.

After reading this, there lodged in Karl's mind and heart the wish to see the ocean at Cannon Beach where he could bring "Elizabeth." *If not Ellie, as I had promised, then her beloved doll whom she had named after her own name. In some sense she had lived through her doll. I must find a way to take "Elizabeth" to the sea shore. . . to the Pacific at Cannon Beach!*

This thoughtful reading from Roland's journal ushered in a turning point for Karl.

PART TWO

In which Mr. Swensen continues with his life

CHAPTER XXI

Elmhurst 1948

Grief over Ellie's death in 1933 had prevented Karl for many years after losing her from writing his account of the blossoming of their love. In that long interval Karl had thrown himself into his work. He had become something of a recluse. Mr. Swensen, who lived and taught in Old Main was an effective teacher and a respected colleague. Little was known of his personal life. He was perceived to be a lonely bachelor.

A few years after Ellie's death, Karl Swensen made a trip to Bozeman to receive his inheritance. He then began to wrestle with the question regarding its disposition. After returning home, the breakthrough came when the realtor he had secured, wrote to say that he had found an interested buyer for the farmland. The offer was close enough to the appraisal figure at the time that Karl's realtor advised him to accept the offer. In time, the deal was closed and Karl instructed his realtor and attorney to meet the banker and place the income in an account under Karl's name at the Security Bank n Bozeman. In the spring of the following year Karl was able to make a trip to Montana and arrange for the renovation of the house on Reese Creek.

But his immediate concern was his teaching, particularly his western frontier course. And a field study idea sparked by his inheritance of the Reese Creek property needed further refining. Because of its relative proximity to the headwaters of the Missouri, so critical in the Lewis and Clark exploration, a field trip to Gallatin County could provide students a first hand exposure to this aspect of the frontier. As Karl expanded upon this idea he realized that other frontiers could also be explored from the Reese Creek location. In time, Karl worked out the outline of a week long field trip to study all six frontiers in the development of the West.

This had led to planning and expediting a major redevelopment of the facilities on the Erickson property to accommodate a small group of students who would come out to study the frontiers. As much as possible, Karl's time was spent on preparing for this much anticipated project.

Every so often Rudolph Bauer ate lunch in the Commons he sometimes sat with Karl. On one occasion Karl was enthusiastically talking about his frontiers field study. Rudolph expressed interest in the project and then asked Karl, "What is it that caused you to specialize in Rocky Mountain frontier history."

Karl pondered his friend's question for a moment. "I lost my birth parents in the 1918 flu epidemic I did not hear much about my family history until I came upon a letter my mother had written me shortly before she died. She told me the story of my grandfather's coming to the gold fields of Montana when he was mustered out of the Confederate army and then made his way into the nearby farming community in which he raised his family. The family which was my own origin. Somehow this gave me my identity of which I have since taken possession.

"I became intensely interested in the development of the Rocky Mountain West of which I now considered myself a son."

"I can understand where you're coming from." Rudolph responded. "I think my teaching German comes from my own pride in my German heritage, which, I guess, is similar to your motivation."

"That's interesting, Rudolph."

With that the two friends finished their lunch together.

In the years since Ellie's death, Karl's life was enhanced by a continuing relationship with Ellie's family and their love for him. They had included him in many of their family gatherings over those years. Mrs. Burgess treated Karl as a son, even at times offering him motherly advice. Mr. Burgess had taken very seriously the legal ramifications of Elizabeth's death, making sure that her estate would fall to Karl. His major concern was that the ownership of the lake shore apartment would go to Karl Swensen.

On one occasion when Karl was spending a week with the Burgess family at their cottage on Lake Geneva, Karl and Mrs. Burgess were sitting on the porch overlooking the lake when she spoke intently to Karl. "I think it is time that you entertained the thought of finding yourself someone whom you would want to marry."

When Karl gave some indication of resistance to such an idea she continued. "You have to be lonely and it isn't right for your grief to take over the rest of your life. As I think about how you must feel, Karl, you should know that if you do find someone, Mr. Burgess and I would in no way feel that you were being disloyal to Ellie or to us. I believe Ellie would want you to go ahead with such a relationship."

Karl was quiet for a while and finally spoke. "It is somewhat overwhelming to have you tell me this. . . I truly appreciate such a caring word to me." Nothing more was said, but Karl would remember this conversation. The impact of this conversation together with the Burgess family relationship which had grown for Karl brought about his readiness to write his story. In the fall of 1948 he began his memoir.

Now for many months he turned his attention to writing his story during his weekend visits to the lake shore apartment. After a number of weekend visits to his lake shore apartment this project came to an end with his heart-wrenching account of his wife's death. After Ellie's death Karl had resolved to make a pilgrimage to the Pacific. In a symbolic way he would fulfill his promise to bring Ellie to the ocean. It would be years before he could make the trip to the coast. And in some ways that pilgrimage would release him from the past as well.

He had other matters to think about. As the end of another academic year approached, the field study project occupied all of Karl's available time. A week after the end of the school, the first field study at the Reese Creek Center would begin.

CHAPTER XXII

Reese Creek, Montana, June 1949

Early on a Tuesday morning in June, Maynard and Dale, along with five other Elmhurst College students, stepped off the westbound North Coast Vista Dome when it came to a stop at the depot in Bozeman, Montana. A small school bus repainted light green with the name "Reese Creek Field Center" on its side was awaiting their arrival. Mr. Swensen met them at the side door of the van. "Welcome to Montana!" He was enthusiastically greeted by them as he helped them climb into the bus. They drove through the north side of Bozeman, and up the Spring Hill Road to the Reese Creek school. Soon they came to a cluster of cottonwood trees in the midst of which was the house of their destination. They turned in at a small sign indicating *Reese Creek Center*. Karl drove up to a barn converted into a garage and stopped the van. "We have arrived." With that he opened the van door and helped his passengers out. He then led them to the front door of the house in which he had spent the first few years of his life.

The house had recently been renovated according to Karl's directions and appeared new with its replaced windows and front door, a new metal roof, and a fresh coat of paint, the same green in which the van had also been painted. A cement path from the driveway led through a newly planted lawn to the front door.

Karl led his group into a small center hall with a stairway leading to bedrooms. To the right was a living room with enough chairs and tables to accommodate group meetings as well as a lounging area. To the left of the entry was a dining area set up for as many as ten or so.

Behind the dining room was a small commercial kitchen, which had been installed up to Gallatin County code.

Karl led the group into the meeting area, where they were then seated facing a fireplace with an Elmhurst College seal above the mantel. In Latin it read *"In thy light, we see the light."*

After the group was seated, Mr. Swensen addressed the group. "Our location here is in the heart of the Gallatin Valley. Among the first documented visits into this area by European descendants was that of Meriweather Lewis and William Clark on their journey to the Pacific. They entered this valley in 1805, coming in from the northeast on the Missouri River and reaching its headwaters twenty five miles or so to southwest of here at Three Forks where the Gallatin, Madison, and Jefferson rivers converge to form the Missouri. On his return, Clark crossed this valley on his way to float the Yellowstone eastward to join Lewis on their return to St. Louis.

"Earlier, Indian tribes had regularly traversed this valley. In the years immediately following Lewis and Clark, fur traders and mountain men such as Jim Bridger and John Colter were often in this valley traveling one way or another.

"After Lewis and Clark and the fur traders had made known this bountiful region, there came families from the east looking for land to settle. Among them was John Reese and his wife, who settled here beneath the mountains which you will see just east of us, one of which is known as Ross Peak, named after Melvin Ross who settled here in 1863.

"You will see when we move about, how fertile the Gallatin Valley is, and why it was called in earlier times *The Valley of Flowers*. It is now populated by many very productive farms, perhaps resulting from early day promoters who called it *Little Egypt*."

Mr. Swensen then introduced the Six Frontiers field study which was to take place during the next week. He then gave the group "housekeeping" details regarding meals and accommodations. At the close of the orientation, he distributed a syllabus by which the "Six Frontier" theme would be carried out.

SIX FRONTIERS IN THE HISTORY OF THE ROCKY MOUNTAIN WEST

DAY 1 Monday

1. **Fur Frontier:** Lewis and Clark, Mountain men 1804-1864
   Tour to Three Forks of the Missouri State Park
   Relationships with Indian tribes
   Jesuit and Protestant Missionaries
   Treaties, Reservations.
   Various presentations of these issues.
   Tour of Big Hole Battlefield (if time permits)

DAY 2 Tuesday

2. **Mining Frontier:** Gold, Silver, Copper, Coal 1858
   Presentation on John Bozeman and the Bozeman Trail
   Tour of Virginia City, and Butte

DAY 3 Wednesday

3. **Livestock Frontier:** Open Range Land and Cattle companies.
   Tour of the Grant Kohrs ranch in Deer Lodge
   Charlie Russell Museum in Helena (if time permits)

DAY 4 Thursday

4. **Agricultural Frontier:** Homesteading, Rail Roads, Towns,
   Agricultural Extension 1900
   Tour of Montana State College Agriculture Building
   Ag. Extension Staff presentation.
   Church extension into newly established towns

DAY 5 Friday

5. **Petroleum Frontier:** Oil, Gas, Refineries 1915
   Tour of Farmers Union Refinery in Laurel

DAY 6 Saturday

6. **Tourism-recreation Frontier:** Hunting, Fishing, Dude
   ranching Tour of Yellowstone National Park1872

Return through the Gallatin Canyon.

DAY 7 Sunday

First Presbyterian Church–Bozeman. Montana–Founded 1872
10 AM Presentation: About Sheldon Jackson and Brother Van
11 AM Worship
12.30 Dinner at the Bozeman Hotel
Free time
Overnight at the Bozeman Hotel

"This will show you what we intend to do this week. You will
note that on most of the coming days, we will be traveling to sites in
which the frontier emphasis of the day can be reviewed first hand.
On Thursday we will go up to Montana State College to hear some
presentations from faculty in Agricultural Extension.

"We will be covering a vast amount of information in six long
days, and so it will be important for each of you to keep fairly complete
notes. As you note what you discover to be the frontiers, make some
observations about both what was gained and what was lost in this
region as it developed over the past centuries. As an example, you will
see when we visit Alder Gulch and Virginia City, that while acquiring
precious metals also the land was lost with the piles of tailings spoiling
the land surrounding the mined areas. While wealth was taken from
the river, productivity of the land was lost.

"Hopefully the travel itself will provide you with some fun and
enjoyment as you enter places and scenery new and different from what
you are accustomed to. Our breakfasts will be here in the Center. Sack

lunches will be prepared for us to carry along, except for Thursday when we will eat in the Student Union Building cafeteria on the college campus. Suppers we will take in cafes on our way back from each tour.

"You will see that Day 7–Sunday-- will be in town at the Presbyterian Church in the morning and at the Bozeman hotel following. The rest of the day is free, as well as Monday morning. Later in the week you may have found ideas for your use of that time. You need to check out together by noon and to be at the Northern Pacific Depot by 1:30 for your departure to return to Chicago."

Mr. Swensen answered questions from the group after which he invited them into the dining room for their evening meal. When the meal was completed he announced, " Feel free to look around the grounds and make your way to bed whenever you are accustomed to turning in. Breakfast is at 7."

With that, the group pretty well stuck together with a mood of eager excitement. Karl retired to his own room upstairs. He checked his notes regarding the week ahead and felt confident that he had prepared the program for the week as best as he could. But he still felt anxious about how this first field study would work out.

On Monday morning the group gathered after breakfast to board the van for their first day of study and touring. In the hour or so during which the group traveled to the Headwaters State Park a few miles north of Three Forks, Montana, Mr. Swensen gave a brief lecture covering the journey of Lewis and Clark. He gave a more detailed covering of their arrival at the headwaters of the Missouri River, the naming of the three rivers which converged to form the Missouri: The Jefferson after the president, the Madison for the Secretary of State and the Gallatin for the Secretary of the Treasury. When they got off the van they could view the way in which the rivers meandered toward the Missouri, and experience the reasoning behind the choice of the Jefferson on which the explorers decide to proceed.

In the evening at the Center, Simon Looking Elk from the Ft. Peck Reservation spoke of the Presbyterian mission in the 1880s and referenced the coming of Jesuit missionaries into western Montana as early as in the 1840s when Father DeSmet arrived from St. Louis to work among the Flatheads.

Tuesday morning, the group remained at the center where a member of the history department of Montana State College lectured on the development of gold, silver and copper mining in Montana. After a coffee break another faculty historian told the story of John Bozeman and the Bozeman Trail. The afternoon was spent touring Virginia City.

After spending the day on Wednesday visiting the Grant Kohrs Ranch in Deer Lodge, group relaxed after dinner while a western country music band performed for them.

Thursday the group spent on the campus of Montana State College. Dr. Robert Dunbar of the history department explained in detail homesteading, with an emphasis upon the need for new approaches which this semi-arid area of the Great Plains required. He spoke of new laws regarding the use of water, the need to develop new farm implements, and revised procedures for raising crops like the development of strip farming in which half of ones land would lie fallow on alternate seasons in order to maximize water use.

Lunch was served in the cafeteria of the Student Union Building. In the afternoon Dr. Merrill Burlingame, of the history department, spoke of the coming of the railroad and the development of towns and other institutions, such as churches and schools.

Friday was spent in Laurel at the Farmers Union Refinery at which various Farmers Union managers explained their processes. Also a review of petroleum development in Eastern Montana and a brief history of petroleum in the Billings area was given.

Saturday was a full day with a trip to Yellowstone National Park entering at Mammoth, where the Park Historian hosted a lunch in the Mammoth Hotel Dining Room where he gave a history of the Park from its very inception in 1872 as the world's first national park. After brief visits to Old Faithful and other major sites, they returned to Bozeman. They traveled north to Bozeman through the Gallatin canyon where they stopped at West Fork to hear an old timer resident in the valley, Dorothy Vick, tell of the beginning of dude ranching in the area. That evening in the Center a representative of Fish, Wildlife and Parks described hunting and fishing in Montana.

On Sunday morning the field center group met with an elder of First Presbyterian Church, Dr. Gene Schilling, who gave a brief history of the origin of the church. "In 1872," he began, "Sheldon Jackson of the Presbyterian denomination organized this congregation in Bozeman, the first of seven churches he would organize in a two week period in what is now Gallatin County, and which was, by the way, the first

Presbyterian church in all of Montana." Elder Schilling went on to tell a few more facts about the church and about Bozeman at that time. He then introduced a member of the Methodist church who spoke of the spectacular work of Brother Van in organizing Methodist churches throughout Montana.

The group then attended worship, after which, Mr. Swensen met with them for their final meal and discussion in the Bozeman Hotel dining room. Mr. Swensen was pleased to receive a unanimous appreciation from the entire group for a very worthwhile experience.

On Monday morning Karl stood on the Northern Pacific depot platform and waved to the departing students after the first "Six Frontiers" field study. The week had gone like clockwork and he felt very satisfied about the outcome. The discussion he had conducted on the return from Yellowstone assured Karl of the success of the study. He was confident that each participant would write a perceptive final essay, which he looked forward to reading upon his own return to Elmhurst.

Karl spent Monday at the Center on Reese Creek tying up loose ends from the week's activities and arranging with the staff for the final weeks of their work for the summer.

CHAPTER XXIII

Karl had other priorities to pursue. Now in western Montana, he estimated that he was halfway to the coast. And he had the time. He resolved to make his way to the sea with "Elizabeth" and to fulfill his promise to Ellie.

He decided that the best way to carry out his mission to the sea would be by car. The next day he asked one of the Center caretakers to drive him into Bozeman in the Field Study van. He found a 1947 Chevy sedan on the used car lot of the local Chevy garage.

The following week, Karl set out on his special pilgrimage to the Oregon coast. He drove to Missoula, Montana the first day and to Spokane, Washington the second. On the third day he dropped down into Oregon and traveled along the Columbia River to Portland. His destination would be Cannon Beach, at which Uncle Roland had his first taste of the ocean, one which had re-directed his life. And in Roland's sharing of his mystical love of the ocean with Ellie, she found life enhancing inspiration as well. Now also Karl had been deeply influenced by Roland's life.

It was late afternoon when Karl reached the edge of the continent and stood on the shore of the Pacific. . . Cannon Beach at long last. He was mesmerized, as wave after wave rolled up onto the sand. . . each one coming from far off on the horizon. What lay beyond the horizon he could only imagine. The Hawaiian Islands–Japan–the continent of Asia and the exotic places Uncle Roland had visited.

Here I am at the ocean where I promised Ellie I would bring her. He had yearned to see this day, to be here with Ellie in spirit.

Alone in this sacred place, Karl drew the doll out of his pocket. He lifted "Elizabeth" to his lips and kissed her. And then he thrust the doll out to sea with all his might. As he did this, he shouted into the crashing waves. **"Bon voyage, Ellie!"** Behind the sound of the next rushing wave he seemed to hear far away words. *G o o d b y e, K a r l, d e a r. . . . Come to me some day. . . .*

He sat down with his back against a sandy rise. The sound of the sea seemed to diminish into a mystical silence. He felt a relieved feeling of calmness. He sensed that now Ellie was at ease with God. He felt that a load of sadness had been lifted from him. In its place a deep sense of anticipation. . . *some day. . . some day. . . some day. . .dear Ellie!*

Later, he had no idea how long he had remained except to observe that the sun was setting over the distant waves when he arose slowly returning to his car. His feeling was one of completion and anticipation, as he usually felt after completing preparation for his next lecture. As he looked down the beach to his left, he saw a woman walking pensively along the wet sand near the water. Karl returned to his tourist cabin. He intended to leave in the morning to return to Montana,

After breakfast, Karl went out to the beach once more. He parked his car and walked down to the place where he had been the day before. However, it felt different. Elizabeth had been with him as he had approached the sea the afternoon before. His promise to Ellie had finally been fulfilled, bringing a profound closure to Karl which he could not yet verbalize.

As he approached the rise where he had watched the sun go down the previous evening, he was surprised to find someone—a woman sitting where he had leaned against the rise. "Oh. I'm sorry. I didn't mean to disturb you," he quickly excused himself.

"That's all right. I think I have taken your spot."

"Oh?"

"I saw you here last night. While I was walking along down there," She pointed to the left.

Karl realized now that she had been the woman he had seen in the distance.

She saw him hesitate and then assured him. "There's room here. Sit down, if you want."

Karl surprised himself by sitting down at some distance from this stranger. "Thank you. I am Karl Swensen."

"How do you do, Karl. I am Grace Edwards." There was a warmth in the way she responded. "Are you from here?"

"No, I am from Illinois where I teach in a college. But most recently I came here from Montana, my original home. And you?"

"I teach at Lewis and Clark College in Portland. . . or I did, that is." She sounded defiant.

"Oh?" Karl did not know if it would be all right to ask further.

She surmised his hesitancy. "It's OK. I guess I needed someone to talk to about it. . . I'm not tenured.. . . and they are not renewing my contract for next year."

"School financial condition? I know a lot of private colleges are having some funding pressures."

"That's what I was told. . .but I think there's more to it." *In fact I know there is.* "Tell me about your college."

Karl could see that the subject had run its course. . . for now. . . and so he described Elmhurst to Grace and what he had been doing on the recent field study.

"That sounds fascinating. What brought you out this way?"

Karl did not want to share anything abut Ellie and the ocean. "Oh, I wanted to see where both the Lewis and Clark expedition and the Oregon trail came to their destinatins at the Pacific. My origins were on the Lewis and Clark trail, and not too far from the Oregon trail in Wyoming."

"I see."

"Well," Karl said as he got up. "I need to be on my way. . .a bit of a drive back to Montana."

"It's been nice talking to you. . . ."

Phrasing it as an afterthought, Karl said. "By the way, here is my card, in case I can be of any help in your re-location."

"Thank you, Karl," she said warmly. "And goodbye."

"Goodbye, Grace."

CHAPTER XXIV

Karl's return to Reese Creek was rapid and uneventful. The staff which he had hired for the week of field study had tidied up the house and left it locked up until its next use would require their services. Karl assumed that the next use would not be until next summer. Certainly he would repeat the field study in another year. He spent a couple of days on the paperwork to close out his obligations to those who had helped with the program. He finally put his car away in the barn and asked a neighbor to take him into Bozeman where he went to the NP depot to await the arrival of the eastbound North Coast Limited which would take him back to Chicago.

After boarding the train, he had twenty-six hours to unwind and assess the experience of the field study. He also thought a lot about his own pilgrimage to the sea. Karl felt that the study would bear repeating on a yearly schedule. He jotted down notes to himself about what changes might be made. He was eager to read the reports from the study participants which would be waiting for him when he returned to his office.

As the train sped across North Dakota in the night, Karl found himself thinking about Cannon Beach and his release of Ellie's doll. Most poignant of all was the realization that he had gotten "Ellie to the sea" as he had promised. *Now everything is Okay.* He also pondered the mystical feeling that someday he too would go out beyond the horizon and once again be with his beloved Ellie. With this thought he fell asleep to the steady rolling of the train.

The next morning he woke up when streaks of light struck him from between the edges of the heavy dark green window shades. He

freshened up in the rest room at the end of the coach and then made his
way to the dining car. He had a quick breakfast of plate sized pancakes.
After his coach passed over the bridge crossing the Mississippi he soon
began to see the familiar sights of Illinois whiz past his window. It
wasn't long before the train was passing through the outer suburbs of
Chicago. His feeling of arriving home was tinged with sadness. Ellie
would not be here to meet him.

The noisy bustle of the inside of Union Station was almost
overwhelming as were the busy city streets as he made his way to the
Northwestern station. When Karl stepped off the commuter train in
Elmhurst and walked briskly to his office on campus, Cannon Beach
slipped into the background treasure house of his mind.

The field study papers from participants were waiting for him in
his office. He spent the rest of his first day back, reading the reports,
which he found very well done. The cumulative effect of his reading
was confirmation of his satisfaction over the first field study. Already
he had begun to envision some adjustments for the second such study.

His phone rang. "Hello, Swensen, here."

"Karl. Welcome back." It was Mr. Burgess. "We'd like you to come
for dinner this evening."

"I'd like that."

"We want to hear all about your Montana trip. . . and also Oregon.
How about 6:30?"

"Yes, that will be good. And thank you so much for thinking of
me."

Karl spent a delightful evening with the Burgesses. He felt so much
at home that it surprised him. He shared enthusiastically his experience
in the field study. Mrs. Burgess would remark afterwards to Ellie's,
father. "I have never seen Karl so animated as when he recounted his
field study experience."

"And such a settled feeling as when he told us about Cannon Beach."

When it was time to leave, Mrs. Burgess hugged Karl and said.
"Come to see us often, won't you!"

"I'd like to, M. . .Mrs. Burgess." He had almost said "Mother."

He returned to his lodgings in Old Main and prepared for bed.
That night he dreamed of Mrs. Burgess and of Ellie.

Early the next morning he was in his office. After winding up the
details of his Reese Creek adventure, Karl turned to preparation for the

courses he would be teaching in the fall. Unlike other summers, Karl found this task dull in comparison to the Montana experience.

From time to time he had opportunity to talk with other faculty members about the study. One such colleague was John Graham, professor of geology, who was exceptionally interested. "I had a similar experience out in Montana, when I was a graduate student at the University of Indiana."

"Is that right!"

"Yes, Indiana has a permanent field station called the Judson Mead Geologic Field Station of Indiana University. It is in the Tobacco Root Mountains, 40 miles southeast of Butte, Montana, and 65 miles west of Bozeman."

"I'd not heard of that. Not too far from Reese Creek where I was. Tell me about it."

"It is owned by the university which has field studies and teaching seminars throughout the summers. I'm not sure about the rest of the year. Probably not. Anyhow it is permanently staffed. I was there for a six week course. It was a great experience—really put me ahead of the game in terms of my preparation for my doctorate in geology. . . besides that—that's where I met my future wife!"

"That's really interesting. I'd like to know more about it."

"You're in luck, Karl. The Field Station Director will be here in October to talk with prospective participants in next summer's studies. In fact, I'll be sure you get a chance to meet him."

"Thanks, John. I'd like that."

As the summer months moved ahead, Karl found himself thinking frequently about the Indiana station and whether or not such a program might be a possibility for Reese Creek. An expansion of the facility and the employment of professional staff would require major funding, In no way could Elmhurst College provide for such a permanent station and program. Perhaps a consortium of Midwestern colleges could be established. There might be grant money available. Or interested donors. He wished Uncle Roland were still alive to consult with. Or Mr. Burgess—did he have that kind of money? Or contacts?

Deep in thought about his future, Karl spent a rare weekend at his lake shore apartment. He had not been there very often since the year before when he had finished his story. When he entered the lobby he was greeted by an unfamiliar security guard. "May I see your identity, sir?"

"Just a moment." Karl reached in his wallet to show his driver's license.

"Thank you, sir." The guard checked the information. "You may go up."

Karl felt like an intruder in the elevator going up to his floor. As he entered this time and took a seat at the lake side window, thoughts of Ellie flooded his consciousness. He realized that so much of his writing in this location had concerned Ellie. Now that she was gone, and long after Roland's use of it, the place seemed uncomfortably empty to Karl. His life had moved on to other concerns.

It was at this point that the idea struck him that if he sold the apartment, the money could go to the field station he had been envisioning. *Something to consider.* But then when he thought about it, he really did not want to let the apartment go.

Soon the familiar routine of the beginning of another academic year took over, and it wasn't long before Karl found himself in class lecturing, in his office grading papers and tests, seeing students, and preparing for classes.

One day in early October, John Graham dropped in to see Karl in his office. "Karl, Lila and I would like to invite you to dinner at our house next Friday when the director of the Judson Mead Center will be with us for the evening. I know you would benefit from hearing him talk about the Indiana center, especially since it is near your place in Montana."

"That sounds good, John. And a dinner with you and Lila would be good whether or not you have a special guest."

"Great. How about 6 o'clock?"

"I'll look forward to it."

On Friday evening Karl walked the short distance to Graham's home on Alexander Street. After dinner Karl joined John and his guest from Indiana in the living room. After some preliminary conversation, Karl was given an opportunity to explain a bit about his western frontier program. Then the Indiana director gave Karl a most helpful explanation of the Judson Mead Center. The discussion covered the advisability of putting a board of directors in place, suggestions of financial grants which might be available, program ideas and advice on food service.

Before Karl took his leave, the Indiana director gave him an invitation to visit the Center sometime during the next summer. "It has been good to meet you and to hear a bit about your first field study at Reese Creek."

"I have appreciated so much hearing about the Judson Mead Center, and I look forward to seeing it in person."

"I am eager to show you around. Just as our location is excellent for geology study and research, I can see that your location fits your western history focus quite well."

With that, Karl took his leave. Karl was now even more convinced of his desire to develop the idea of a full summer of study and research at the Reese Creek Center.

CHAPTER XXV

May 1950

Since the beginning of the academic year the previous September, Karl Swensen had, in effect been engaged in two full time jobs. He had a reduced teaching load of two courses, and was engaged in the major task of planning and developing the field center out at Reese Creek.

He had consulted with the college administration to suggest that the Center be made an official program of the college, similar, as he had explained, to the relationship of the Mead Center to the University of Indiana. The college board had agreed to this arrangement. However, the financing of the center would be the responsibility of its own board.

Karl's planning had been greatly assisted by his contact with the Indiana station director. His first priority had been the development of a board of directors of the new center. The newly formed board of directors then developed funding for the project, through obtaining grants from some of the sources Karl had been given by the director of the Mead Center.

One of the board members, a retired Bozeman general contractor from Bozeman, was overseeing the expansion of the facility. Another board member, who was on the history faculty of Montana State College in Bozeman, worked with Karl in the development of an initial six week series of field studies for the first summer season which was soon to begin.

At the conclusion of the academic year Karl Swensen was in his office immersed in reading term reports and other end-of-the-year work. With commencement a week away another academic year would

soon come to an end. He was excited at the thought of the first year of
the field center. But the development of a full time center would keep
Karl at Reese Creek as it's director for the full year. This made him sad
to think that he would not be teaching classes at Elmhurst. He would
miss his family relationship with the Burgess's. And in a way, Elmhurst
itself.

However, it was with keen anticipation that Karl looked forward to
his trip out to Montana in two weeks, after marching in the academic
procession. Karl thought about all this as he leaned back in his desk
chair when his phone rang. "Hello, Mr. Swensen speaking."

"Hello Karl. This is Grace Edwards. Remember we met out on
Cannon Beach?"

"Certainly, Grace. How are you. Good to hear your voice."

"I was afraid you might not remember me."

"Oh no. In fact I have wondered whether you had found another
teaching position."

"Well, I have. . . sort of."

"How is that?"

"I have a part-time temporary job at Whitworth College in
Spokane. . . a couple of courses just ending this year. Don't know yet
about next year." She seemed to hesitate. "That's why I thought I'd
call. . . to see if you know of any openings."

"No, but then I'm out of the loop. I am to leave Elmhurst to work
full time on a project I have initiated in Montana. I told you about the
field study we did last year there. Well, I am expanding this idea and
have formed the Reese Creek Field Study Center."

"You have!"

"We plan to sponsor seminars and research opportunities all summer
long with a fully staffed facility for resident participants and staff."

"That sounds intriguing, Karl. But isn't it a bit scary just starting
up from scratch?"

"You've got that right! But exciting just the same. Program and
research ideas keep popping into my head. I know we can't do everything
right off, but I'm looking ahead."

"Well, Karl, I can see that you are in your element and I wish you
the best in this venture."

"Thank you, Grace. . . and I hope you will find something soon.
Let's keep in touch. Let me have your address or phone number."

"Yes, let's." She gave him her contact information before they finished their call. "Good bye, Karl."

"Good bye, Grace. Thanks for calling."

Commencement was a bittersweet ceremony for Karl. He saw it as marking the ending of a productive and enjoyable career as history professor at Elmhurst College. But it also was ushering him into a new career with a set of new experiences as he prepared to take on the role of Director of the Reese Creek Field Study Center near Three Forks, Montana.

While parents and friends flocked to greet and congratulate graduates after the recessional music concluded, Mr. and Mrs. Burgess hurried up to surround Karl Swensen, their "son," with their love and good wishes. Mrs. Burgess was beaming. "Karl, we are looking forward to a commencement dinner in our home at six o'clock! We hope you can join us."

"I'll be there for sure."

"And then we have invited the folks you designated for something of a party afterward!"

"Yes—the field study participants and the new Board members. . . can't wait!"

The dinner was very special and the party couldn't have been more memorable for Karl. Maynard and Dale were the last to leave. Karl stopped them at the door for a word. "Dale. What are your plans?"

"I'll be enrolling in Eden Seminary in St. Louis in the fall. I'll help Dad on the farm for the summer."

"My very best to you, Dale."

"Thank you, Mr. Swensen. I have enjoyed being in your classes."

"Maynard. Your degree is in business management, isn't it?"

"Yes it is."

"Do you have a position yet?"

"No, I haven't found anything yet."

"How would you like to go out to Montana and take the position of business manager of the study center?"

"That would be out of this world! You mean it?"

"I do, but it's not out of this world—but almost!"

"Wow!"

"Come to my office in the morning and let's talk about it."

"Thank you, Mr. Swensen."

"It's *Karl* now!"

The next day when Maynard Otterberg arrived at Mr. Swensen's office Karl greeted him enthusiastically. "Maynard! Welcome to the Reese Creek Field Center staff!"

"Hello . . .Karl."

"I want to share with you what we plan and what is yet to be arranged, before we get into what I anticipate to be your responsibilities as business manager."

"I'm eager to hear about the Center."

"Good. In some ways, if you were to imagine what we did during our week of field study last summer as one of a series of weeks throughout the summer, with varying programs you would be able to envision in part what we plan. To begin with, we are set up as a not-for-profit corporation with a board of directors. Some members are from this region, others are from Montana. I am responsible to them to carry out the program and policies which we have agreed upon. The board has obtained the capital needed to expand the facilities as well as to establish investments from which to subsidize the current budget for the first few years of operation."

"Wow! That's quite a lot, I imagine."

"Yes, it is. The work on the facilities is almost completed. It is mainly the addition of a dining hall and kitchen added to the original house, and building four separate cabins capable of housing twelve participants in each. One of the cabins will be all-weather, with a kitchen to accommodate staff.

"So far as staff is concerned we plan to have a building and grounds manager, and a food service manager, as well as business manager. My responsibility will be program."

"Does that mean that we will all be staying on the grounds?"

"Not necessarily. We'll see whether the work requires it in each case. I should think that in your case, you could live in town somewhere and keep eight to five hours, so long as you had someone on site as registrar. In fact, I am toying with the idea of establishing a year-round office for myself in Three Forks, and possibly a residence."

"Why Three Forks?"

"I like the idea of identifying the center with the Lewis and Clark discovery of the confluence of the three rivers making up the Missouri. For your office, the architects have remodeled one of the upstairs bedrooms into a business office. The remainder of the original house has been redesigned for meeting space of various sizes. . . that's about it for now. . . any questions, Maynard?"

"No, except regarding a time line for the start-up."

"I plan to get there June first, and I'd like to have the full staff assembled by the fifteenth of June, when we plan a dedication and open house. Will that work for you?"

"Yes."

CHAPTER XXVI

Reese Creek–1950

The newly graveled parking area was filling up with cars. Visitors entering the grounds were welcomed by a board member. "We have volunteers here ready to show you around, not only to the main house but to the other facilities. And as you have a look at the cabins, I might note that each cabin is named after an early day town in this immediate area. *Hamilton, Bridgeton. Gallatin City* and *Anceney*".

After viewing the cabins, the visitors entered the main building to see both floors of *The Erickson House,* the original home. Finally the visitors gathered in the new *Elizabeth Burgess Dining Hall* where they were greeted by Mr. Swensen, Director of *The Reese Creek Field Study Center.* It was the day of the grand opening and dedication of the Center.

Karl had struggled long and hard to compose his dedicatory remarks. When all had gathered, he stood up before the assembled group with all of the board members seated on the front row waiting for his words. After giving a concise history of the development of the Center, Karl introduced the board members of the Center, Dean Mueller of Elmhurst College, and staff managers. "And finally I want to introduce the two Bozeman architects, "Bill Graybo and Paul Schofield who have helped us to design this fine facility which we now dedicate."

After applause, Karl continued. "And now we dedicate this Reese Creek Field Study Center to the discovery and dissemination of the truth of the history of the Rocky Mountain West and its current circumstances. We especially dedicate the Erickson House in memory of the original homestead family on this property and we dedicate the Elizabeth Burgess Dining Hall in loving memory of Elizabeth Burgess, class of 1930 of Elmhurst College." Karl paused to hold back his emotions. We have invited Dale Schmidt. Class of 1949, Elmhurst College to offer the dedicatory prayer.

Dale rose to offer the prayer of dedication: "Almighty God who dost enlighten the minds of Thy servants with knowledge of Thy truth, let Thy blessing rest upon this Reese Creek Field Study Center and upon all who study here and upon those seek truth and teach here. May the work done here be to Thy Glory and to the advancement of humanity. For *In Thy Light we see the Light.*" Amen

With that, the program drew to a close and refreshments were served to an enthusiastic audience. Karl was surrounded by well-wishers as the crowd began to disperse. None of these kind words were more appreciated than those of the Burgess'es. "Elizabeth would be so proud of you, Karl. We are so honored to have her memory kept in the name you have given to this fine dining room." Mrs. Burgess said as she gave Karl a hug. "But remember my advice and my wish for you to find someone special for you again."

"Yes. I'll try and remember. . . but I have to get this thing we have just dedicated rolling successfully first."

Contrary to earlier limited expectations, the first summer season was a full one with research projects and study sessions scheduled from immediately after the Center's dedication through the end of September. Overall it was a successful start to this new venture. But, of course there were glitches here and there as the managers and staff adjusted to the realities of having to serve groups of participants and keep the facility running smoothly.

Karl found that his having to attend to a constant barrage of details made it difficult for him to guide and direct the total thrust of the season and to think beyond it to the coming year. Karl sought out one of his local board members with whom he had consulted in the development of the center. He was manager of the Sacajawea Hotel in Three Forks. Karl frequently had lunch with him in the hotel dining room. In early August, Karl brought up his frustration to his friend and board member. "I am so inundated with minor problems that I can't seem to attend to the overall program."

"What do you mean by the overall program?"

"I feel that I ought to be relating to each program or research director to evaluate our effectiveness in serving their needs. . . and this would help me in my planning for next year."

He thought about this for a while and then suggested. "I think you need an assistant director to follow the immediate details, allowing you to see the big picture."

They talked about this for some time. "I see what you mean, and I think I do need to find someone for an assistant." Both men needed to get back to work, but that conversation would help Karl in more ways than he could at that point imagine.

When Karl returned to his office, Maynard, who had been covering the phone in his absence notified Karl of a long distance call from Spokane he had missed. Karl phoned the number Maynard had left for him. "Hello, this is Grace Edwards."

"Grace this is Karl Swensen. You called?"

"Yes, Karl. I called to let you know that I will be in Bozeman next week to interview for a position at Montana State College."

"Sounds wonderful."

"Well, not as good as you think. Another part-time one . . but maybe with more potential than the one at Whitworth which has ended for me."

"I'm sorry."

"Don't be. I needed something different. Anyway, what's the chance of seeing you? Then I can explain further."

"Yes I'd like that."

"They will be putting me up at the Baxter Hotel next Monday evening after my interview—could you meet me?"

"Good, Why don't I meet you there for dinner. Would six o'clock work?"

"That's good, Karl—6 o'clock."

"O.K. Good-bye for now."

"Bye."

Karl returned to thinking about his conversation with his board member. *An assistant could be the person who works directly with the leadership of each of the research projects and study seminars. . . a sort of host getting the participants settled and taking care of day-to-day needs as each event progresses. Up until now, these responsibilities have eaten up all my time and energy. Having an assistant really would help.*

Karl sat down with Maynard to determine if the budget could afford at least a part-time assistant. Full time appeared feasible. He took up the idea with a couple of the local board members. They were reluctant but thought that the idea could be tried out during the remaining two months of the first season. As Karl pondered this possibility, he questioned whether such a person could be found on such short notice. The answer was closer than he thought.

Karl drove into Bozeman late Monday afternoon and met Grace Edwards waiting in the lobby of the Baxter Hotel.

"Grace. Good to see you again."

"Yes, Karl."

"How'd the interview go?" he asked as they were seated in the dining room.

"They have offered me a part-time appointment for the fall term, which looks pretty good—a bit more than I had at Whitworth."

"Sounds good."

"But nothing now for the summer."

Karl thought about that and almost blurted out. "So how about coming to work at the center. I need an assistant during the rest of the summer."

"You serious?"

"Yes, I am. The fact of the matter is that we have just come to the conclusion that I need an assistant to free me up for a more general oversight."

"Well, I don't know. It is such a new idea and I don't know enough about it."

"Well, it is new to me too. It is something we would have to work at to determine what you would be doing. . . but you need to see the Center and we need to talk about how it would work. Are you here long enough to have a look with me tomorrow?"

She thought about this for a bit. "Yes, Karl, I could stay. In fact I'd like to see the Center no matter what."

"Let's do it." By this time they had finished their meal. "But now, this evening let me show you around Bozeman."

"OK!"

They left the Baxter together and Karl ushered Grace into his car. Karl showed her around Bozeman, including the college and residential areas near the campus. Their conversation turned to more personal matters. "Have you always lived in Oregon and Washington?"

"Yes, I grew up in a little town in eastern Oregon and went to college at Oregon State in Corvallis. And you?"

"Montana. Born in Reese Creek, raised in Billlings. Graduate school at the University of Chicago."

For the rest of the short tour each filled in some details about their interests and various experiences. When they returned to the Baxter Hotel, they finalized arrangements for Grace to see the Center in the morning.

The next morning Karl picked Grace up at the Baxter and they drove out to Reese Creek in time for breakfast in the dining room. Karl then led Grace on a tour of the Center and its facilities. As they toured, he explained as much as possible about the programs underway.

Karl could tell that Grace was very much intrigued with the Center and its program. By the end of her tour and an interview with Karl and Maynard, she gave her answer. "I would very much like to accept your offer and to come on board as assistant director."

"And we very much want you to join our endeavor."

Maynard added with an uncharacteristic smile, "And I look forward to working with you, Grace."

Afterward Karl would think *Maynard's interest seemed a bit more than business-like. . . that cuts me out if I ever I had similar thoughts.*

Grace Edwards' coming onto the Center staff worked very well for the balance of the Center's first year. At the close of the summer program Maynard and Karl met with Grace and it was determined that she would stay on as the assistant director. In this way she would be involved in the development of plans for the succeeding summers.

The Center program grew in the years following Grace's addition to the staff, giving Karl time and opportunity to develop and promote the program. While the Center remained under the sponsorship of Elmhurst College, its reputation grew to interest students and faculty from other colleges and universities, particularly those in Montana. A close relation grew with Rocky Mountain College in Billings and Montana State College in Bozeman. To enhance this wider interest, a history faculty member from M.S.C. as well as a member of the Rocky board had been invited to serve on the Center board.

A waiting list of students wanting to take part in seminars developed, leading the board to consider the need to expand its facilities. Maynard developed contacts with sources of grant money which would be expanding this segment of the center's income. Grace exceeded Karl's expectations as a assistant director in charge of the ongoing program.

In the course of all this successful work during the next few years, Maynard and Grace grew very close. Much to Karl's surprise, they invited him to dinner at the Baxter in Bozeman one Friday evening. Between the main course and the dessert, Maynard said to Karl, "We have some news we would like to share with you before making a public announcement."

Karl replied with a knowing grin. "What is that, may I ask?"

"We plan to be married in the fall after the Center program has concluded."

"I think that is the best news of the season—though not entirely unexpected!. . . where will your big event take place?"

Grace answered, "In Elmhurst in the College Chapel. Maynard has told me so much about Elmhurst."

"That's wonderful."

CHAPTER XXVII

Elmhurst, October, 1955

Autumn colors were illuminated on the campus with a bright afternoon sun as Mr. Swensen mounted the steps into Irion Hall. A small crowd had already gathered in the chapel while the chapel organist played an assortment of pieces. Karl made his way into the lounge where Maynard Otterberg, dressed in a dark gray suit, nervously awaited the coming ceremony. At about the same time the Rev. Dale Schmidt entered the room dressed in his black clerical gown with a white stole.

They greeted one another somewhat solemnly. "Are you ready?" Dale asked. The other two nodded and Dale began their procession into the chapel. Dale led, followed by Karl and finally Maynard. They entered the chapel and walked to the front. Dale took his place in the center facing the congregation. On his left was Karl and then Maynard.

The organist shifted to the familiar bridal processional. The congregation stood and turned to watch the maid of honor, a close friend of Grace's from Oregon, come forward to take her place opposite Karl. At that point, the bridal march music increased in volume as Grace Edwards came down the aisle on the arm of her brother, James. Maynard stepped forward to meet her. Her brother then sat down in a front pew.

As Karl, Maynard's best man, watched Grace walk toward the front, he felt a slight tinge of envy when he saw how beautiful she looked in her white linen suit, carrying a bouquet of flowers, with a radiant smile as she approached Maynard. Karl remembered how he had experienced the beginning of romantic feelings for Grace when they had begun working together. But he reminded himself that he had put those feelings away as he renewed his silent pledge to Ellie.

The wedding was followed by a reception in the Commons. As Karl left Irion Hall and began to walk toward the Commons, he glanced up ahead to Old Main and felt a rush of nostalgia. He entered the reception line and offered his sincere well wishes to Grace and Maynard. Soon everyone joined in the send-off of the newlyweds whose honeymoon would be their return to the Montana they both had come to love.

Among the guests were the Burgesses, who were eager to approach Karl. "Karl, we want you to join us for dinner in our home this evening if you are free."

"I'd like that very much." Karl felt a sense of relief, knowing how alone the wedding had made him feel.

"Come down as soon as you can, Karl."

"I will, thank you."

Karl left the campus and walked down Prospect under the arches of beautifully colored autumn leaves. Again he was overcome with a feeling of having returned home, a feeling which intensified when he sat down in the Burgess living room to await dinner. Over the past five years since the Reese Creek Center had become his full time position, he had not been back to Illinois. The college had allowed him to store his possessions in his locked up office in Old Main. He had sublet his lake shore apartment under the management of the building.

Now having returned to Elmhurst, he found himself not looking forward to spending the fall and winter months in his Three Forks apartment and office preparing for another summer season at the Center. *I have to admit—I miss teaching.*

The dinner was a "down-home" meat loaf supper – nothing fancy. Karl felt like a member of the family and was treated as such. After the meal, Karl helped clear the table and dried dishes while Mr. Burgess retired to his home office to do some work. This gave Mrs. Burgess a chance to chat with Karl. "I thought maybe you and Grace would have hit it off."

"To be honest, I had a little of that feeling at first. But it was like a "No admittance" sign kept me at a distance."

"Oh? How was that?"

Karl was reluctant to explain. "It is kind of hard to say. . . ."

"You don't have to tell me."

"No. . . I'd like to. . . I heard a voice–in my imagination, I'm sure-- but a voice. . .It was Ellie calling, *Come with me, Karl, to the sea. . . .*"

"Oh, Karl, dear!"

"It was then I knew. . . that I will always belong to Ellie."

Mrs. Burgess did not want to press Karl any further and so changed the subject. "When do you have to return to Montana?"

"I need to return for a Board meeting at the end of the month. But I have to admit. I don't look forward to it as I should to the beginning of another year. . . ."

"Oh?"

"Being here in Elmhurst after such a long time has sort of gotten to me. I have an odd feeling that this is really where I belong."

"Karl, that's not so odd. After all you have become a part of our family."

Karl thought about this. "Yes, *Mom*, I have." He continued. "I remember when Ellie invited me to come to your cabin on Lake Geneva. I was pleased and so glad to be with her for a few days, but so apprehensive about meeting her family and worrying that I would not be accepted. And then when you burst out of the front door to greet me in such a warm and receptive way, I was suddenly freed from my reluctance and I knew everything would be okay. And it has been much more than okay. Though of course we all miss Ellie so much. It still hurts."

"Oh Karl" Was all she could say. But her smile and her hug said it all

PART THREE

*In which Mr. Swensen
finds his home.*

CHAPTER XXVIII

Reese Creek --January 1956

The Center board gathered in the Center lounge for its annual planning meeting. Karl was joined by Maynard and Grace to report to the board. Maynard gave a full financial report showing a balanced account of the previous year and a budget projection for 1956. "You will notice that our income projections cover our anticipated expenses."

Karl gave a report of Grace's assistance throughout the year, noting his total satisfaction with her work. Karl then gave a summary of his work throughout the previous year with particular emphasis upon plans for the 1956 season.

The board members had a few questions regarding each of the staff reports. They showed their appreciation for the work which Karl had reported as well as their approval of plans for the current year.

After a brief pause to allow the board to rest easy about the coming year, Karl spoke. It was at this point that Karl presented his own intention for the future. "I have made the decision to step down from the directorship of the Center as of April 30th. I believe without a doubt that Grace Edwards is capable to taking over the lead position. I have discussed this with her and she is willing and eager to take over if you give her that opportunity. My reason for stepping down has nothing whatever to do with the Center or with the board support you have provided most abundantly. It is rather my desire to return to the college classroom. I have spoken with my dean at Elmhurst and she is ready to put me in the classroom beginning in the fall of this year.

Board members were quick to offer their appreciation to Karl Swensen for his pivotal role in the development of the Reese Creek Center. Many expressed their understanding of Karl's desire to return to teaching. Many expressed their regret. The board took action to accept Karl Swensen's retirement from the directorship and to confer with Grace Edwards regarding her willingness to take over. With that, Karl's final Center board meeting was adjourned.

Karl spent the next three months working with Grace and Maynard in preparation for the coming summer program. He then closed out his office and apartment in Three Forks. At the end of April, the Center board and staff held a farewell reception for Karl. He was greatly gratified by all the appreciative words he was given.

On April 30th, Karl Swensen boarded the Northcoast Limited in Bozeman bound for Chicago. After placing his carry-on items at his assigned coach seat, he climbed the narrow steps up to the Vista Dome to take a seat there to watch Montana recede into the West behind him. Four hours later, having passed through Billings, Karl was moved by the thought: *I have a most unusual feeling. . . almost like I am going home. . . and yet rationally I don't know where my home really has been.*

May 1956, Elmhurst, Illinois

Karl moved back into his former apartment in Old Main in the week before commencement, in time to take his academic gown to the cleaners before putting it on for the first time in years in preparation for the academic procession the following Saturday.

During the week he found great pleasure in reconnecting with old associates and in meeting faculty and staff who had come to the college since he had left to work in Montana. He was especially happy to share with John Graham the success of the Center. Karl wanted Graham to know of his crucial part in the Center's development. "The day you dropped into my office and told me of the University of Indiana field station was the key that opened this particular jewel box, John!"

"Well, all I did was to point to the Mead Center."

"But, that was all it took!"

Soon commencement weekend arrived with many proud parents and friends on campus for the occasion. On Saturday afternoon everyone assembled in the Gymnasium. The band played "Pomp and Circumstance" as Karl marched with the faculty up toward the podium, followed by the candidates for the bachelor's degree. Karl knew none of the students, and only some of the faculty, yet he felt at home in this setting which he recognized as his college. He smiled to himself as the college president conferred the Bachelor of degrees ending with the ponderous phrase which always delighted him . . . *with all the rights and privileges appertaining thereto.*

After the ceremony he walked through the clusters of proud parents and joyous graduates to make his way back to Old Main. The sight of proud parents caused a familiar but unwelcome shadow to creep across his consciousness. He thought of his stepparents. They had been with him the day he received his bachelor's degree from Eastern in Billings. They had been proud. But in the years following his departure from Billings, he had drifted apart from them. Possibly this was due to the fact that they had discouraged him about his decision to go to Chicago for a masters' at the University of Chicago. There was, however, the pleasurable Christmas they had spent together when he had found out about his inheritance. Then, when they had retired and moved to Iowa there had been little contact except for an occasional letter or card. Six years earlier, when he had informed them about the dedication of the Reese Creek Center, they had sent a note of congratulations, but said that they would not be able to come to Montana for that event. *I guess occasional correspondence is all that is left. If I am honest with myself, this is just a continuation of the feeling I always had of not quite feeling fully at home in Billings.*

He walked slowly and pensively. But then he turned his attention to the campus reveling in every view: the overarching Elm trees with their light green leaves of spring, carefully cut lawns, the well worn steps into Irion Hall, and stately Old Main with its echoes of decades of classes.

He entered Old Main and climbed the steps to the third floor. In his old familiar office and apartment, he shed his gown once more and hung it up, to be taken down next year. He relaxed in his desk chair, knowing that Monday he would need to begin in earnest his preparations for teaching next fall. He checked his watch and rose to prepare for the festivities with the Burgess's. He left Old Main and made his way down Prospect to the Burgess home for supper. *Home for supper!* He mused. *Home at last.*

As it turned out, his supper with the Burgess'es would be weekly, usually on Wednesday evenings. These were welcome breaks in Karl's routine during the summer of spending most of his time in his office and in the library preparing for a full teaching load in the fall. But it was work which he enjoyed. He took pleasure in anticipating teaching once again.

The lease to whom he had rented his lake shore apartment ran out at the end of July, and so he was able to spend some of his weekends on Lake Shore Drive in August. On these occasions he enjoyed reading passages from Uncle Roland's journal. He found one of these especially pertinent.

Whenever I am asked where my home is, I am hard put to know how to answer. I left my parents' home when I was eighteen to join the Merchant Marine. So much has happened in my life since then that I hardly remember much of my childhood home in northern Michigan. My whole life, it seems, has been aboard one ship or another. But home has to do with being with loved ones and in certain beloved places in one's life. When I think of it in these terms, home for me is being with my sister in Elmhurst.

As Karl re-read this he reflected on Roland's words he thought to himself. *Home for me is Elmhurst.*

Not many weeks later, after Karl had been back in the classroom, the returning alumni descended upon Elmhurst College for the homecoming weekend, the yearly renewal of friendships and memories. On Friday afternoon former students began arriving. Karl was thrilled when Maynard knocked at his office door around four o'clock. "Maynard! And Grace! I didn't know you were coming!"

"We didn't either, but the closer the time came, the more we wanted to." Maynard proclaimed. Then Grace added. "The board settled the matter when they suggested we come and they offered to pay our way. This will give us an opportunity to report personally to the college board."

"I think that's great, and before the weekend's over we must get together," Karl responded. Maynard added. "And I'll invite Dale and his wife too.

"By all means. I didn't know they were here as well? How about dinner out tomorrow night? I would like to suggest the Spinning Wheel at 5:30 on Ogden. Know where it is?"

"Yes, we will look for you there at 5:30." Maynard replied.

"Good, but let's also get together at the Alumni Dinner tonight." Karl said.

By 6 PM there was a substantial gathering of alumni for a special dinner and a program in the Commons, in which the president welcomed everyone and gave a glowing update of the college's progress over the previous year. The Alumni secretary recognized returned graduates by year and announced where each of the special year's classes would gather, beginning with the tenth year group and ending with an acknowledgment of the three fiftieth year alumni who had returned.

The president then introduced faculty members who were attending the dinner. He ended his introduction with a special word. "And finally we welcome the return of Mr. Swensen who has been off campus these last five years out at the Reese Creek Center in Montana." Karl stood and everyone applauded. "And, Karl, I wonder if you would be willing to share something about the Center? Not all of our alumni may know about your work there."

This took Karl by surprise, but the subject was so close to his heart that he had no trouble speaking about the Center. After giving a brief explanation of the Center and its program of study and research, he told of his retirement from the directorship, and then took great delight in introducing Grace and Maynard Otterberg as the Director and Business Manager of the Reese Creek Center.

The dinner and program adjourned with the singing of the Alma Mater.

> Where the elms in stately glory,
> Spreading branches raise,
> There our cherished Alma Mater
> Hears our song of praise.
> School we love, Elmhurst,
> Live for aye
> God shed His grace on thee.
> Loyal be thy sons and daughters
> To thy memory.

Karl was especially moved when the alumni sang the Alma Mater at the close of the day's festivities. He would speak of this in chapel on Monday.

Homecoming was well on its way with the parade the next morning and the football game in the afternoon. Elmhurst lost to North Central from Naperville. Some would say, "According to custom."

The dinner with Maynard and Dale and their wives at the Spinning Wheel was an especially nostalgic evening for Karl, not only because being with Maynard and Dale brought back his earlier days as their teacher and leader of the first Reese Creek seminar, but because it brought back memories of Ellie and Karl at the Spinning Wheel. Moments of emotion would keep him from speaking.

After Dale Schmidt graduated from Eden Seminary in Webster Groves, Missouri, he had been ordained and installed as pastor of a small church in eastern Iowa. Much to Karl's pleasure, Pastor Koch of St. Peter's in Elmhurst had asked Dale to preach the sermon on Sunday morning of homecoming week end. When Dale heard that Karl had the Monday morning chapel service at the college, he and his wife decided to stay through Monday.

On Monday the campus settled back to its usual routine. Thus, in mid morning most of the student body was seated in the chapel including many of the faculty as well. Maynard and Dale and their wives also were also in attendance when Mr. Swensen stood at the pulpit and offered his heartfelt remarks about the meaning of *Alma Mater* as the *mother who nurtures* us. "When we leave our parents' home to come to college, we enter a new home, in that the college itself nurtures us as a mother. His scripture and sermon affirmed the Christian concept of the fatherhood of God. It is God who most fully nurtures us. "In a sense this means that the Christian is at home with God. Similarly we find ourselves at home here at Elmhurst. That's why so many return home here each year for homecoming."

The morning chapel service concluded with the singing of the Alma Mater.

On the steps of Irion Hall Mr. Swensen bid good-bye to Maynard and Dale and their wives. As he walked toward Old Main he thought to himself. *Where the elms in stately glory—spreading branches raise. . . . here I have indeed found my true home.*

EPILOGUE

In which Mr Swensen is remembered.

October 1999

Maynard kissed Grace good bye at the door of their home in Three Forks and began his short drive to the air terminal just east of Belgrade, Montana. He would be boarding a Delta flight to Salt Lake City and on to a connecting flight to O'Hare in Chicago.

The afternoon before, as he had left work at the Reese Creek Center, he very carefully cut a small branch with yellow leaves from a cottonwood tree next to the main house. He thought of the first time he had seen the house at Reese Creek with massive Ross Peak in the background. He thought of Mr. Swensen with love and appreciation for him which had grown through the years. How the course of his life and that of Grace's had been transformed by Karl Swensen!

Maynard boarded his Delta flight carrying a plastic bag which held the cottonwood branch. He was returning to Elmhurst for the fifty-year reunion of his class. When he arrived in at O'Hare in Chicago he was met by Dale at the arrivals gate. The two old friends hugged briefly. Dale drove to a nearby motel for Maynard to check in before the two drove the short distance to Elmhurst College.

After a nostalgic and enjoyable two days of homecoming, Maynard and Dale made a special visit to the Elm Lawn cemetery on Lake Street before leaving Elmhurst. They stopped in at the office to ask for the location of the grave they wanted to see. They found the marker they were seeking.

They stood before it in awe. Each quietly read what had been engraved on the granite stone.

MR. SWENSEN

Reese Creek, Montana 1914   **Elmhurst, Illinois, 1986**

Sunset and evening star,
And one clear call for me!
And may there be no moaning at the bar
When I put out to sea.
Twilight and evening bell. . . .
I hope to see my Pilot face to face,
When I have crossed the bar.

---Alfred Tennyson

Maynard knelt and placed upon the base of the marker a small cottonwood branch with its yellowed leaves of fall from the tree next to the house at Reese Creek. Dale quietly offered a prayer of benediction. As the two old friends turned to leave, they stopped abruptly when they read the name on the stone next to Mr. Swensen's.

ELIZABETH BURGESS SWENSEN

Elmhurst, Illinois, 1914   **Chicago, Illinois,1934**

The buoyancy of the sea will carry me home.

–Roland Whitaker

After years of wondering, the two old friends, members of the class of '49, looked at each other with an understanding of Mr. Swensen's life story at long last.

AUTHOR'S NOTES Mr. Swensen and those with whom he is associated are products of my imagination. However, the settings in which this story takes place are as real and as historically accurate as I have been able to depict them. All that remains of Reese Creek is the abandoned school house and individual farms in the area. The convergence of the three rivers forming the Missouri can be seen, as originally discovered by Lewis and Clark, at the Missouri Headwaters State Park about 35 miles west of Bozeman. To achieve as much historical and geographical accuracy as possible, the work of the late Robert Dunbar and the late Merrill Burlingame, historians at Montana State University, have been most helpful to me, as has the writing of Phyllis Smith in <u>Bozeman and the Gallatin Valley</u>. However, references to Elmhurst College and its surroundings were to be found in my own memory from my student days at Elmhurst from 1945 to 1949, the period during which much of this story takes place. And, by the way, the chapel organist who plays in this story is real. John Schroeder, my roommate in college and good friend ever since, was one of the chapel organists at Elmhurst College in our time there. The scenes from the Oak Park Arms Hotel are from my memories of having been a bellman at the Arms during my high school, college, and seminary days.

ACKNOWLEDGMENTS

I am especially indebted to Kurt Schoening, my brother-in-law, whose nostalgic watercolor painting of Old Main on the Elmhurst College campus appears on the cover. I also acknowledge my friend, John Shellenerger, whose photograph of a deserted and dilapidated house not far from Reese Creek became the model for my depiction of Karl's early childhood home as well as for references to this house as the story develops.

Once again I am thankful to Jody McDevitt, my daughter-in -law, for her editing skills. As in the past my son, Dan, has provided me with essential technological assistance in submitting my manuscript for publication. And I am thankful to my wife, Doris, for her encouragement and editing assistance.

Finally I thank Kevin Laguno and Alyssa Richter of Xlibris for their help in bringing MR. SWENSEN into published form.

PREVIOUS NOVELS BY PAUL KREBILL
A Place Called Fairhavens
Harry's Legacy
Heritage Hidden
Moriah's Valley
Westbound
Return to Arrow River
Sylva
U-Turn
Trails' End

ALSO BY PAUL KREBILL. . . . .
WORDS For Thinking and THOUGHTS
For Meditation. . . 366 Devotionals
The Cowboy Bob Treasury, children's read-aloud stories

Printed in the United States
By Bookmasters